He is Watching

Denise Carbo

To my son Alex, a gifted artist and a wonderful young man. I am so proud of you and full of love and hope for what the future holds in store for you.

Chapter One

A cascade of photographs tumbled across the computer screen, interrupting the design Julie Roy had been working on.

Pictures of her.

Images of her at home in her apartment, a favorite coffee shop, the grocery store, in her car, and at work, sitting at her desk exactly as she was now.

The pencil clenched in her hand snapped in half. Heart racing, Julie peered over the short wall of her cubicle and scanned the entire room. A few dozen similar workspaces filled the center of the large open area with management offices lining the perimeter. A couple of people mingled near a tall, fake, potted plant. Most stared down at their desks or computer screens. No one appeared to be paying her any attention.

A phone rang. A metal drawer clanged shut. A stapler clicked in the cubicle next door. The sounds were like symbols clashing together in her head. Harsh breaths beat a staccato of sound as panic overwhelmed her.

Rolling the desk-chair forward, Julie slapped at the power button to shut down the computer. The screen cleared and darkened to black, but the invasive images remained burned into her mind.

Her stalker was back.

Julie snatched up her cellphone to call the police but dropped it into her lap as tears pricked the backs of her eyelids. *What was the point?* She'd reported each incident of pictures in her mailbox, slipped under her door, and under the windshield wipers on her car. They had no leads. They'd been courteous, but less than encouraging about finding the person responsible.

Evidently, she didn't rank high enough on their priority list for the cops to get out and actually look for the stalker.

Jerking to a standing position, she jumped when her chair rolled back and hit the wall. Her gaze darted around the room. Megan, one of her coworkers, gave her a hesitant smile before turning back to her work. Julie grabbed her worn, brown, leather backpack from the floor while repeatedly casting her gaze around the room. *Could it be someone here at work? Watching her right now?*

Other than a quick glance, everyone ignored her and focused on their own workstations. She slipped her drawing tablet and paperwork for her current project into her backpack and stuffed her cellphone into the side pocket. Julie slung the pack over her shoulder and searched the room one last time.

She had to get out of here.

She sidestepped a co-worker as she strode to the elevator and kept her gaze glued to the floor. Pushing the button repeatedly, she swung around with her back to the door and watched everyone in the room. The elevator pinged its arrival at her floor. Julie jumped, and her breath caught in her throat. She peeked over her shoulder as the doors opened into the empty silver box. Sighing in relief at finding no occupants, she stepped in and pushed the button for the parking garage. Normally she took the stairs because of a mild case of claustrophobia, but today the lack of multiple exits and opportunities of someone lurking in wait superseded her fear of small enclosed spaces.

The doors began to slide closed, but a hand sliced between them, forcing the doors to open wide. Gripping the strap of her backpack in her fist, she held her breath.

Jack, a co-worker, stepped inside and nodded in her direction before leaning against the back wall.

The breath left her lungs in a whoosh, drawing his gaze. Her stalker couldn't be Jack. She'd known him for a few years, since she started working here. She had even set him up with her friend Diane. They'd only gone on a couple of dates before both moving on, but it ended amicably. It couldn't be him, could it?

"Bit early for a lunch break, isn't it?" *Lunch break?*

He signaled to the instrument panel and the highlighted garage button she had pushed.

Yeah, it was a little early, but she couldn't stay here another minute, and eating lunch was the last thing on her mind.

Julie shrugged her shoulders. Let him think what he wanted.

Wait. Where was he going? He hadn't pushed a button when he entered the elevator.

She stared at him nonchalantly slouching against the wall. His dark brown hair was a bit long and overdue for a trim. Jack's dark gaze glanced up from the phone in his hand to the illuminated numbers of the floors above the doors and then to her. His eyes narrowed.

"You sick or something?"

"You didn't push a button. Are you going to the garage?" If he was, she certainly wasn't.

"Oops." Jack stepped forward and pushed the button for the second floor. Human Resources was on that floor. Should she report the pictures on her computer screen?

Yes, probably, but it would have to be by phone. She needed out of this building now.

"So, what's up with you? Sick or not? You look pale."

Should she claim an illness? She certainly had physical symptoms. Her head was pounding. Her stomach churned.

"You ever figure out who was sending you pictures a while back?"

Julie's throat closed. She wedged herself farther into the corner and clenched the handrail.

How did he know about the pictures? Why was he mentioning them now? Was it him?

"Diane said they really spooked you." Of course, Diane. She knew about them.

Julie cleared her throat. "I didn't realize you and Diane still talked." Diane hadn't said anything about him, but then again, Julie hadn't talked to her in weeks. Or anyone else.

"We hang out once in a while."

He stared at her expectantly, so she nodded.

"Who was it?"

"What?"

"The pics? You know who it was?"

"Oh, no, I don't, but the police are looking into it."

"The police? For some pictures? A bit of an overkill, isn't it? I mean, they're probably from some guy crushing on you."

The elevator stopped and opened on Jack's floor. He stepped out and glanced back at her as the doors closed.

He thought she was overreacting. Or did he say that because it was him and he was trying to minimalize what happened and throw her off? Jack had never acted interested in her. He never flirted, and he wasn't the shy type so if he had been interested, he would have shown it or flat out asked her out on a date.

Was she overreacting?

She couldn't tell anymore. All she knew was her entire body was telling her to flee.

When the elevator arrived at the underground garage, she leaned her head out the open doors, searching in every direction for anything out of the ordinary. The wide, round, cement pillars and rows of vehicles became suspected hiding places. The elevator door alarm sounded. Lurching forward, she stumbled over the threshold. A car started. A door slammed.

Not caring what anyone might think, she sprinted to her little green sedan three rows away. Gripping her keys in her tightened fist, she stabbed at the lock on her car door frantically until it finally slipped in. Julie yanked open the door and jumped into the seat, slapping down the lock switch.

Her heart pounded, the sound drumming in her ears. Hyperventilating, she clutched the backpack to her chest.

What was she going to do? No way could she sit around waiting for her stalker to slip up and get caught or no longer be content by terrorizing her with pictures.

Maybe then she would become a priority for the police. Assault and battery case? Sure, move on up the list. Rape? Murder? Ding, ding, ding, congratulations, you've now reached the top of the pile.

Dropping her forehead to the steering wheel, Julie clenched her eyes shut. She needed to escape. Quality sleep had eluded her for months. Fear and panic had moved in and taken over her life. She'd overslept this morning, so instead of riding the T to work, she'd driven.

One thing she could be thankful for. Standing and waiting for the T to arrive while people surrounded her was the last thing she could endure.

She tossed the backpack onto the passenger seat, put on the seatbelt, and shoved the key into the ignition. A day or more out of the city might clear her thinking. She would tell no one her destination, or even that she was leaving. Sadly, only her coworkers or boss were likely to notice her absence. She had become a hermit over the last six months. Shutting herself off from friends hadn't been intentional, but socializing and going out had become too scary to handle.

On the way to her apartment building, she thought of and discarded a dozen different destinations. She and her parents weren't particularly close. They spoke a few times a year around the holidays and birthdays, but that was all. They had always lived their own lives, never knowing what to do with the surprise-late-life-baby who had burst into their well-ordered world. Julie had no siblings or other close relatives.

Approaching her building, she searched for an empty parking space. It was always a gamble whether she would be lucky enough to find one within a few blocks of her apartment. It being the middle of the day worked in her favor, and she spotted an opening. After parking, she remained in the seat for several moments. Cars sped by, people hustled down the sidewalk, customers entered and exited the fast-food place and convenience store across the street. No one appeared to glance in her direction.

Julie grabbed her backpack and jumped out of the car. A garbage truck drove by, dragging with it the stench of decay. She jogged down the sidewalk to her building. Not meeting anyone on the stairs, she held her keys at the ready and jammed them into the locks of her door while her gaze darted over her shoulder. The door swung closed with a shove, and she flipped the locks closed and slid the chain across. The locks shown with polished brightness as only new metal could. She had replaced the aging original lock and chain and added two more after the first onslaught of pictures arrived.

Leaning back against the locked door, her gaze searched the small one-bedroom apartment. A small kitchenette occupied the corner with yesterday's and this morning's dishes piled in the tiny stainless-steel sink. Housework hardly topped her list of fun activities, but lately exhaustion prevented her from caring about dirty dishes. The overstuffed, secondhand, navy couch and recliner she'd acquired from a college roommate when they'd left without paying their share of the rent took up the remainder of the room.

Her roommate, Carla, had combed through Julie's belongings, purloining anything she coveted for herself on a regular basis. Not paying the rent or helping with any of the cleaning chores had been the last straw. She had confronted Carla, whose volatile response ended in her throwing a mug and several dishes at Julie's head. When she had come home from work the next day, her roommate was gone. She'd downsized to this one bedroom after that fiasco and vowed to have no more roommates.

Once this had been her haven, her first home all her own to do with as she pleased, but now she realized safety was an illusion. Someone had been inside her apartment and had taken pictures of her unaware. The police hadn't found a hidden camera, but how else had the pictures been captured?

They hadn't searched hard enough.

Julie dragged a wooden stool across the floor to the wall separating her bedroom from the living space. It scraped against the hardwood floor, making her cringe over the obnoxious screech. She peered into the narrow air vent, searching for a hidden camera.

Nothing.

Leaning her forehead against the wall, she swallowed the lump in her throat and blinked away the threatening tears. She didn't know if she was disappointed there wasn't a camera or terrified someone had been inside her apartment taking the pictures when she wasn't home.

Oh God! What if she had been home at the time, sleeping or showering? Could they have been inside watching her?

Sprinting into her bedroom, she started shoving clothes into her backpack. Suitcases alerted anyone watching of her intention to flee. She paused, biting her lip. Her rent was paid through the month. Thankfully, her bank gave her the ability to pay any remaining bills online. She remembered hearing somewhere credit cards were traceable, so she needed to stop at the ATM and get as much cash as they allowed her to withdraw.

She slipped a sketchbook and an assortment of pencils into her backpack. Julie went nowhere without drawing supplies. Grabbing toiletries from the bathroom, she crammed them into the last usable space in her bag and latched the top.

Her skin crawled as she remembered the picture of her lying on her couch. He'd tainted everything here. *How had it been taken? From where? Were they watching her even now?*

Perspiration dampened her skin. Every instinct she had was telling her to run. Hoisting the backpack over her shoulder, she left the apartment without looking back. She didn't know when or if she would return. She only knew she couldn't stay here.

Chapter Two

The little gas pump icon had flashed on several miles back, and at any minute Julie expected it to start blinking and beeping—warning the car was running on fumes. The exits had grown farther apart and so had the signs advertising any amenities like gas. Leaving Boston, she had driven for hours and still had no destination in mind. She had taken the first highway on-ramp closest to her apartment and continued in that direction, passing into New Hampshire and then crossing over to Vermont. She remembered a family ski trip to Vermont as a child. It was the one and only time her parents, who were avid skiers, had taken her with them. She had broken her leg and never attempted to ski again.

It was the middle of September and the leaves were transforming. The farther north she traveled, the more colors she saw. Soon, Fall's spectacular show would be in full swing. Vivid shades of yellow, red, orange, and green spread over the hillsides of New England like a multi-hued carpet.

A sign with icons for gas, food, and lodging appeared. *Finally!* The sign reminded her it was already past dinnertime and she had skipped lunch. A soft growl from her stomach prompted the need for something to eat. Raindrops splashed against the windshield in an ever-increasing amount. She grimaced, peering at the ominous gray clouds up ahead. Looked like it was time to find a place to stay for the night as well. She didn't relish driving in an unknown area at night during a storm.

Taking the next exit, she followed the sign for gas and spotted a set of fuel pumps in front of a small convenience store. She made the turn and stopped at the pumps. Julie grabbed her wallet, and after a quick scan around the empty parking lot, dashed inside the small, white building.

An older gentleman with a thick white mustache stood behind the counter. He gave her a slight nod in greeting. Giving him a half-hearted smile, she glanced at the interior of the store. A single cooler was tucked in between a row of shelves along the back wall. Another row around chest high divided the room. A variety of products, ranging from windshield washer fluid to bags of chips, filled the space. The stale scent of tobacco wrinkled her nose.

She opened her wallet and studied the contents. Her bank ATM had only allowed her to withdraw one thousand dollars, which left her with a grand total of fourteen hundred and eighty-nine dollars and whatever change she dredged up from the bottom of her back-pack or from in between the seats of the car. The greatest expense would be lodging. She needed to conserve her cash to avoid using her cards. Perhaps paranoia had set in, but she wasn't taking any chances. If her stalker could access her work computer, who knew what infor-mation they might get and use against her.

Julie handed the man forty dollars. An assortment of pamphlets advertising local attractions hung out of a clear plastic shelf next to the register. One for a place called the Monarch Inn grabbed her attention. A picture of a three-story, green, Federalist-style mansion with a wraparound porch set amidst a backdrop of dark green moun-tains dominated the advertisement. Folding the pamphlet in half, she tucked it into the front pocket of her pants and took the receipt he held out.

"Thanks."

Jogging back to her sedan, she opened the door and tossed her wallet onto the seat before filling her tank. The narrow aluminum cover over the pumps did not provide adequate coverage from the torrential downpour. By the time the pump shut off, the rain had drenched her to the skin. After climbing back into the car, Julie pushed her wet bangs out of the way and stretched across the seats to grab a handful of napkins from the glove compartment. She wiped her face and chilled arms before starting the car and turning on the heat. It had been a warm day when she left the city, but now she wished she had worn a jacket over her peach silk shell. The cold, wet material clung to her, making her shiver.

Julie glanced at her backpack and rubbed her arms. Had she packed a sweatshirt? She couldn't remember, but she didn't want to dig through the contents to find it now. Besides, it would only get wet too.

She lifted slightly to yank the damp pamphlet from her pants. After plugging the address of the inn into her phone's GPS app and seeing it wasn't far, she pulled out of the parking lot and sent a prayer up that they had a vacancy and were within her budget. Cold, wet, and tired, she needed a place to regroup and figure out what she was going to do. Her stomach let out an irritated rumble. She winced. She really hoped the inn served food, too. She had meant to grab a water and something to snack on at the store but had gotten distracted.

A sign announced she had entered the Mad River Valley. Julie snickered. Mad—both definitions of the word were appropriate for her.

Her abrupt departure from the city bordered on crazy. Angry didn't begin to cover how she felt. Pissed off was a bit closer. The more she thought about her unknown stalker, the angrier she got. Yes, terror still dodged her every move, but she welcomed the rage. The stalker hadn't beaten her. This trip would allow her to regroup and come up with a plan to take back her life. She was done waiting to see what his—or her—next move would be, or if the police would catch him. She simply couldn't continue to live her life in fear and limbo.

Crossing over a river, she turned onto Main Street. A large white church loomed ahead. Julie peered through the frenzy of the windshield wipers and driving rain. A town square with a white gazebo in the center passed by on her left. She had only a vague impression of a handful of local stores and other businesses lining the street before her GPS announced she had arrived at her destination.

Julie spotted a square sign displaying the name Monarch Inn through the rain and sighed in relief. Unclenching her fingers from the steering wheel one by one, she followed the sign for parking and found an open space on the far side of the lot. She stuffed her keys and wallet into her backpack, grasped the handles in her fist, took a deep breath, and opened her car door. What she wouldn't give for an umbrella right now.

As Julie made a mad dash for the entrance, her black leather flats splashed through a puddle. By the time she reached the door, her toes made squishing sounds inside her shoes.

She stepped into the entrance and paused. She must resemble a drowned puppy. Water dripped from her nose, and she blew it away with a huff of breath.

"Oh, you poor thing, come on over here."

Julie blinked through her water-spiked lashes at the man behind the counter. He held out a white hand towel toward her. She squished over to the registration desk.

"You really got caught in it, didn't you?" He gave her a white tooth smile which crinkled his startling blue eyes.

"Unfortunately, yes." She took the offered towel to dry her face and arms. "Thank you." She glanced behind her at the soggy trail she'd left and grimaced.

"Oh, don't worry about that. It's just water. Are you checking in?"

"Yes, please."

"Do you prefer the second or third floor? I have openings on both.

The one on the second opens onto the side porch. The one on the third does not. That one has only the fire exit onto the portcullis roof. Both have views of the mountains."

Closer to the ground with an available exit seemed the more sensible solution. And how sad was that she needed to think of those things? "I'll take the second, please."

"Great choice. I'll need a credit card and your license, please."

Julie nibbled on her lip. Of course he did. You couldn't stay anywhere anymore without providing one. Even if she paid cash, they needed a credit card on file in case of damages. She had no other choice. She sent a prayer the stalker didn't know how to trace credit cards. Retrieving her wallet, she handed over her license and credit card. She wouldn't stay longer than she needed to. And she would pick a different direction when she left.

He dangled an old-fashioned brass key. "Top of the stairs. Take a left. If you're hungry, the Red Maple Café serves dinner until ten o'clock. They serve breakfast from seven until nine in the mornings."

"Thank you. Right now I just want to get warm and dry. After that I'll contemplate food."

"Don't blame you a bit. My name is Conner, and if you need anything at all, let me know."

She smiled and hung her backpack over her shoulder. Turning for the stairs, she stopped. A man strolled down the hall from the café. He was a few inches taller than Julie, with curly brown hair, tan skin, and brown eyes with creases at the corners from smiling a lot or being out in the sun. As she stared, those creases deepened, and a smile spread across his face. A dimple appeared and then another.

Julie cast her gaze to the floor, hunched her shoulders, and hurried to the stairs. She had no interest in a man, handsome or not.

Chapter Three

Joe spotted the woman who'd checked in last night speaking quietly to a little boy. Both were crouched in the sitting area on the second floor of the inn. His lips twitched. Quite a difference from the adorable wet mess standing in the hall last night. She'd pulled her brown hair back into a ponytail. The ends were brightly colored. It looked as if she had dipped her hair into a bucket of blue paint. He liked that look on this woman and couldn't help but admire the way worn denim jeans and a yellow top hugged her curves.

His eyebrows pinched together, and he frowned when she swiveled slightly on the balls of her feet. Dark circles rested beneath her haunted brown eyes.

She glanced up and spotted him standing in the hallway, watching. Her body jerked and then stilled. A fleeting expression of panic crossed her face. The fearful reaction to his presence made his gut churn in sympathy for the woman, and anger toward whoever had caused the instinctual reaction. He smiled in an effort to reassure her.

"Good morning. What have you got there?"

She stood and glanced toward the stairs and then back toward Joe.

The boy looked up from the sketch pad across his lap. "Look at the dragon she drew!"

Joe inspected the drawing. His eyes widened. He had expected to see a caricature or cartoon. Instead, he found himself staring at a fully detailed ferocious looking dragon ready to leap off the page.

"You're awfully talented."

She shrugged her shoulders and mumbled, "Thanks."

A door opened, and a couple stepped out. "Brian, let's go."

The boy frowned and stood. "I gotta go."

She ripped the drawing from the pad and handed it to him with a tender smile. The boy's face lit up.

"I can keep it?"

"Of course."

"Wow, thanks!" He ran over to his parents waiting at the top of the stairs. "Look, isn't it awesome?"

They both eyed the drawing. "It's wonderful."

The woman smiled as Brian waved and the trio descended the stairs. She bent to grab her pencils off the floor. Once finished, she stood and took a step forward, as if to walk past him.

"I'm Joe. Joe Bascomb." He held out his hand.

She glanced down at his extended hand and bit her bottom lip. Shifting the pencils to her left hand, which held the sketchbook, she briefly grasped his hand. "Julie Roy."

"Are you only passing through our lovely town or are you planning to stay a while?"

Julie gazed longingly between the stairs and the door to her room. She had been returning to her room after eating breakfast in the café when she spotted Brian pouting in the small sitting area. He had been sitting on the floor with his arms wrapped around his knees, staring at the rug. The murmur of raised voices coming from one of the rooms across the hall from hers brought back memories of when she was a child. Her parents had gone through a period of fighting loud and long when she was young. It had halted when her father moved out one day without any explanation. He had come back several months later. Again, without a word. Suddenly, he had been part of the household once more. The fighting had stopped after that, or they had gotten much quieter. She had never dared to ask either parent what had happened.

Entering her room, she grabbed her sketchpad and pencils and walked back out to the hallway. The little boy still sat hunched over against the wall. His light blond hair brushed the top of his arm as he rested his head on folded arms across his knees. His big brown eyes spotted her.

She smiled. "Do you like dragons?"

He glanced between her and the door to his room.

"Do you mind if I sit?"

He shrugged, so she walked over to the sitting area and perched on one of the chairs and started sketching a dragon flying with its wings outspread and mouth opened wide in a roar. She saw him peeking at the paper out of the corner of her eye. He let out a gasp as she started filling in the details.

Julie added shading and then showed him the drawing. "What do you think? Should we add him breathing fire?"

He swiftly nodded.

She smiled and added flames shooting out of its mouth and then handed him the sketch pad as she crouched in front of him.

"Here, how about you add the rest of the scene? Do you like castles?" She handed him one of her pencils. He stared at the sketchpad.

A tingling at the back of her neck announced a presence nearby,, and she glanced up.

The man from last night stood in the hallway, staring. Was he a guest of the Inn? Did he work here? It wasn't feasible for him to have followed her here. He had been here before she arrived and dry as a bone. It wasn't possible for him to have snuck into a different entrance to make it seem like he had arrived earlier. Her brain scrabbled at any possibilities and scenarios and rejected every one. He wasn't her stalker.

Still, she wasn't going to leave the little boy and run to her room, so Julie remained in place as he smiled and talked.

Once the parents arrived and Brian left, she grabbed her things and intended to leave too, but he introduced himself. She didn't want to be rude.

"I'm just passing through."

"That's a shame. Autumn Valley has a lot to offer. I'm sure an artist as talented as you could do justice to our beautiful town."

"Do you work for the Inn?"

"No. I make and repair furniture. Kyle, the owner, asked me to check a few of his pieces."

"But you were here last night."

"That's because Kyle is a talented chef and I like to take advantage of those skills every now and again by having dinner in the café."

"Oh, the food is delicious." Julie had eaten in the café last night after settling into her room and changing out of her wet clothes. She had devoured her meal.

She took another step forward.

"Where are you headed?"

Julie blinked and looked at her door.

"You said you were just passing through, so where is your destination?"

Why did he want to know? Why all the questions?

"I haven't decided yet."

"Well then, how about you let me show you around town? Kyle doesn't serve lunch. I can show you the best places to eat besides the Inn. How about it? Can I buy you lunch after a tour of the town?"

Staring at his handsome face smiling down at her, it dawned on her he was actually flirting with her and asking her out. It had been so long she was obviously out of practice.

Shockingly, a part of her wanted to say yes.

"I can't, but thank you."

She sidled past him and strode to her door. She briefly glanced at him standing in place with his hands on his hips, watching her before entering her room and closing the door.

Chapter Four

Julie leaned against the white gazebo railing and gazed around the town square. The sun, presently high in the sky, bathed her face in light and warmth. A couple meandered along one of the brick walkways hand in hand, while an elderly woman sat on a bench. A red cardinal perched on a branch of an elm tree, and the sweet aroma of recently cut grass filled the air. Closing her eyes, she savored the clean scent. It had been quite a while since she had experienced pure country air and the quiet. It was a bucolic scene and her fingers itched to capture it in a painting.

Almost two years had passed since the last time she had painted anything. Her paints were tucked away back home in her closet.

Opening her sketchpad, she loosely sketched the scene. She had intended to be on her way today, but looking out the window of her room at the beautiful mountains and charming grounds, she decided to stay.

At least for one more day.

Aimlessly wandering New England didn't appeal to Julie, and she had no idea where to flee to next. A day or two here might give her a clue what to do with the shambles her life was rapidly becoming. Perhaps she might buy a small set of paints and do a painting or two. She'd like to do one of the Monarch Inn and the mountains and perhaps one of the river as well. An inquiring guest had asked about a covered bridge in the area. Exploring a little of the surrounding sites shouldn't be too risky.

"Fancy meeting you here."

Julie whirled around, clutching the pad to her chest.

Joe stood with one foot resting on the bottom step. He raised both hands with palms facing outward in the air. "Easy. I didn't mean to scare you. I saw you as I was walking by."

"Hey, Joe." An elderly man called out from the sidewalk. Joe dropped his hands and faced the gentleman.

"Hi, Walt. Out for a walk?"

She stuffed the pencil into the back pocket of her jeans.

The man and the golden lab he held on a leash ambled over. Joe crouched and rubbed the dog behind the ears. Tail wagging, tongue hanging out, the dog plopped down and leaned its weight against Joe. He laughed as he almost lost his balance.

"You're one of her favorites." Walt chuckled as his dog lay down on the ground and presented her tummy for Joe to rub.

Joe obliged and gave her a few last pats before standing up. The man wandered off with his dog, and Joe swiveled back toward the gazebo.

Didn't she read somewhere once that if a dog liked you it must mean you were a good person?

He tilted his head and smiled. "Did you decide to stay in town a little longer?"

"Actually, yes. The sun shining and seeing the town in the bright light of day rather than a torrential downpour gave me a new outlook. I didn't relish the idea of getting back in a car, so I thought I would take a walk." She shrugged. "Here I am."

"The offer to show you around and buy you lunch still stands. I know most of the town's best spots and the general area for that matter. I grew up in Burlington, an hour north of here. Interested?"

"What are you, the welcoming committee or something?"

A pair of adorable dimples winked in his cheeks as he grinned. "I don't believe we actually have a designated committee, but most folks are the friendly sort around here. We're proud of our town and like to show it off."

Julie glanced around the park. What harm could it do to listen to his spiel about the town? She was interested, and it wasn't like she had anything planned, which was part of the problem. He might provide a needed distraction allowing her mind to come up with a strategy. The offer of lunch was a bonus. With her limited funds she had intended to skip the meal.

"Okay, as long as it's a walking tour." She wasn't about to get in a car with anyone. Paranoia clung to her strong enough to ensure she avoided being alone with him. He may not be her stalker, but he was still a stranger and for all Julie knew, a serial killer. Didn't they always turn out to be the unassuming neighbor nobody suspected?

"A walking tour it is." He bowed slightly and held out his arm for her to join him on the brick walkway.

She nibbled on her bottom lip. Was she making a mistake?

His deep brown eyebrows rose. "Change your mind? I'm harmless. I swear. I can provide references if need be. My family still lives in Burlington. My parents haven't made their annual migration to Florida yet. Would you like to talk to my mother for her recommendation? I should warn you, however, if she hears I'm taking a woman out to lunch she might start planning a wedding. She's desperate for more grandbabies. You would think my brother and sister kept her well supplied in them. I always seem to be overrun by nieces and nephews at family gatherings and holidays."

A smile twitched her lips. "I don't think that will be necessary." She walked down the steps to stand next to him.

"Are you sure?" He held out his phone. She scanned his screen. Joe stood in a picture surrounded by people bearing a strong family resemblance.

They were all smiling broadly.

She couldn't remember any photos with her in them except the one of her sitting on her mother's lap. Her father stood behind them with his hand on her mother's shoulder. The picture sat in a silver frame on the piano in the living room amidst a slew of photos of her parents on various trips around the world.

Shaking her head, she looked across the street at the tall, white Congregational church. Joe ambled along the walkway, and she fell into step beside him.

"Valley Food and Pharmacy is across the street. If you're in mind for snacks or in need of any toiletries, that's the place to go. The credit union here on our left is convenient if you need an ATM. Not sure if you'll get charged fees or not though if you're not a member. Random Books & Antiques and Trinkets & Souvenirs are across the way if you're looking for anything along those lines. You have anyone at home you want to buy a souvenir for? Family? Boyfriend?"

Julie glanced up to see him smiling at her. "That's not terribly subtle."

Joe chuckled. "Can't blame a guy for trying, can you?"

"None of the above."

"No family?"

"I have family, just no one I intend to buy anything for. We're not close."

She gave him a sideways glance. He frowned as he looked ahead down the street. It was probably hard for him to imagine not being close to family if that picture was anything to go by. "There's no bad blood or anything, we just have nothing in common. My parents had me later in life, and I didn't fit in any mold they wanted to put me in. We're just very different people with different interests."

Joe fiddled with the loose change in his jeans. Keeping his hands in his pockets might seem less threatening. Her hunched shoulders, and the way she was nibbling on her bottom lip again radiated nerves.

The slight indent in the center of her lip made him think it was a long-term habit.

If his father were here, he'd be reminding Joe of his penchant for wounded animals.

It was obvious she was defensive and a bit self-conscious of the distant relationship she had with her parents. He still talked to his parents and siblings pretty much every day. If he didn't speak to at least one of them, it would surely raise a family alarm.

What about birthdays and holidays? Did she not spend them with her parents? He hoped she didn't spend them alone. His chest ached for her, and he rubbed the spot while he tried to think of something to say that didn't sound like he pitied her in any way.

He couldn't imagine celebrating anything without being surrounded by his entire family. Each birthday was celebrated with a party whether young or old. Every holiday the family would get together at his parents' house with extra tables set up to accommodate them all. It was loud but full of laughter and love.

"Folks are different, that's for sure. Not everyone sees eye-to-eye on everything. We each must find our own path. My own had its stops and starts, and a few hard turns, but I think I've found it now."

"You mentioned you make furniture, right?"

Joe smiled. "So, you were paying attention. I went to school and got a business degree and was working in sales." He shrugged. "I was making decent money and figured that's what I would keep on doing. One day after I delivered a set of chairs I had made for my parents, my father sat me down and said I was wasting a gift I had been given. I had no idea what he was talking about and said so. He told me he could see my job brought me no joy but making furniture did, and I owed it to myself to see if it could also support me. He handed me a check for a fair amount and said this should get you started."

He would be forever grateful to his father for setting him on the right path. His former job had brought him none of the fulfillment making furniture did. Sure the money had been nice, but he was steadily increasing his business and his profits. More importantly he was following his passion and building something he could be proud of.

"That there is the Autumn Valley Gazette. We may be a small town, but we have a weekly newspaper that keeps us informed of local events." He pointed to the building as they walked past.

"Obviously you accepted his offer and opened your business, but where did you learn to make furniture if you went to school for business?"

"I had taken woodworking classes in high school and it became a hobby. I expanded on it in college while taking all the electives I could find. The rest resulted from a lot of trial and error."

Julie sidestepped a woman pushing a little kid in a stroller as they meandered along the sidewalk. Joe nodded at another passerby. A good half a dozen people had greeted him during their short walk. He was a popular guy.

Joe pointed to the building just ahead. "Sunny Springs Café has a nice lunch menu. You want to eat here?"

"Sure, you're the expert."

They proceeded inside and sat at a small table for two by the front window. A curvy woman with dark skin and eyes and dressed in a purple wrap dress called out, "I'll be right with you and your friend, Joe."

He grinned, and she couldn't help but stare at his dimples. "I want to sketch you."

He blinked and then leaned back with a laugh. "Um, okay."

Julie leaned over to grab her sketchpad and a new pencil from the backpack she'd dropped on the floor next to her chair.

"Right now?"

She peeked up at him. "Is that a problem?"

He shook his head with a smile. "I guess not. No one has ever asked to sketch me before."

The waitress approached with a pair of laminated menus and placed them on the table. "How you
all doing today?"

Joe gave her a wide smile. "Hi, Tara. This is Julie Roy. She's staying at the inn."

"Nice to meet you, Julie. Welcome to Autumn Valley."

Julie smiled faintly as she smoothed a fresh piece of paper.

"Can I get you two something to drink?"

Joe glanced her way, and she scanned the menu briefly for the beverage section. "Sweetened iced tea with lemon please."

"Sure thing, and for you, Joe honey?"

"I'll have the same."

"Okay, be back in a jiffy."

Grasping the tip of the pencil she sketched the shape of his face. She used deeper strokes along his jaw and then began to add lines for the length of his nose. A slight bump in the bridge made her curious. "How did you break your nose?"

"Hmm? Oh..." He looked up from the menu and chuckled softly. "My sister did it when we were kids. I was trying to teach her how to properly swing a baseball bat, and I didn't get out of the way fast enough."

"Ouch."

"Yeah, it hurt like a ...well, you get the picture."

Tara arrived with their drinks. "Wow, you've got quite the gift there, honey." She gazed at Joe and back to the sketch. "It looks just like him."

Joe peeked over the table, but she shifted it out of his line of sight. "Not yet. You have to wait until it's done."

Tara chuckled. "That's it, make him wait. Do you all know what you want to eat?"

Julie glanced up and then down to the menu she hadn't read yet. "Um, I'll have the chicken sandwich please."

"Burger for me, with fries."

"I'll have fries too."

"Coming right up." She took the menus and sauntered back toward the kitchen.

Julie wondered if Tara would let her sketch her as well. She looked back at her pad and started shading the eyes. They were always the hardest part to get just right. Once you captured someone's eyes the rest fell into place.

"So, is this a hobby or profession?"

Glancing up at him, she frowned. He gestured at her pad.

"Oh, both I guess. I'm a graphic designer but sketching and painting are what I like to do in my spare time if I have any. Although it's been awhile since I painted."

"I don't think anywhere in town sells artist paint, but Waterbury's not far and you should be able to find what you need there. Besides, there's a Ben & Jerry's there and what's a trip to Vermont without a stop for an ice cream sample? We could drive over for dessert and pick up painting supplies for you. Or, if you prefer, take a drive up to Burlington. I know a handful of places that sell artist's supplies. We could drop in and say hello to my parents. They'd love that."

He winked at her and a laugh bubbled up her throat.

"Persistent, aren't you?"

"With things that matter I am."

Their food arrived and Julie alternated between taking bites of her sandwich and fries and filling in the broad details of the sketch. She would finish the drawing later, but she wanted to capture his likeness before they parted ways. Joe continued to tell her about the town, probably to entice her to stay awhile. He tossed in a personal question now and again, but she evaded answering by shrugging or turning the conversation back to him. There was no point in encouraging his interest.

As the waitress cleared the table, Julie stuffed her sketchbook back into her backpack.

"How about another stroll to work off lunch and make room for dessert? We can grab an ice cream."

"Thanks, but I'm going to head back to the inn. Thank you for lunch and the tour of Autumn Valley." Julie stood and hefted her backpack over her shoulder. A tinge of regret shadowed her words. Part of her wished she didn't have to refuse his invitation. She had enjoyed Joe's company.

"Hey, what about showing me the sketch? You said I could see it when you were done."

"Oh, of course..." She put her backpack down on her empty chair and pulled out the sketch book. "It's not exactly finished. I still need to fill in some of the details."

Julie turned to find Joe standing behind her. She startled and an involuntary gasp left her lips.

Joe kept smiling and held out his hand to look at the drawing.

She handed it over and took a small step back to rest her hand on the back of the chair, trailing her finger over a small crack in the wood.

He bent his head and studied the sketch.

His smile dimmed a little but remained. Did he not like her work? She started tapping her finger against the wood. Art was subjective. Not everyone would like a piece or even interpret it the same way.

Knowing that and watching someone inspect your work were entirely different things.

Joe glanced up from the sketchbook and met her gaze. "I can't even imagine having this kind of ability to look at something and make it come to life with paper and pencil, in so little time too."

A sigh escaped her. He liked it.

"Thank you."

He handed her the sketchbook. "You know, there are plenty of picturesque places around here I could show you. I know people too if you'd like to do more portraits."

Julie put away the drawing and picked up her backpack once more. "I'll keep that in mind." She felt his gaze as she walked to the door of the café. The urge to look back at him halted her movement at the door.

Would this be the last time she saw Joe?

The thought saddened her, but she pushed open the door without looking back. He would be a pleasant memory to reminiscence about and smile. She'd had precious few of those lately.

Chapter Five

"*What are you doing in Vermont?*"

Julie gawked at the text message from an unknown number on her phone. Her breath stuttered to a stop in her chest. Her skin iced over. She had told no one where she was going.

She started to shake.

The stalker must have traced her credit card. They knew the number. *And now they knew where to find her.*

"You can't run from me, Julie!"

The phone fell from her hand and bounced on the sidewalk. Hyperventilating, she gaped at the cellphone resting face up on the ground—the message still displayed on the screen. Grabbing a landscaping rock from the garden bed in front of the shop she had been walking past, she smashed the phone repeatedly until the screen splintered. Tears pooled in her eyes, and her lips trembled. What was she going to do? Where could she go?

Snagging her broken phone, she tossed it in a nearby garbage can and headed back to the inn just short of a jog. The stalker could be on their way here now, or possibly already here, watching her. Had he or she been following her and sent the text to see how she reacted?

Frantic, Julie looked around in every direction. A half-dozen or so people walked the sidewalks, and some aimed a few curious stares her way.

The stalker could be anyone, anywhere.

She approached the inn intending to run once again. She didn't have a destination in mind, but she wouldn't stay here waiting for them to act.

Heavy metal music blasted from the speakers. Sawdust danced in the air and coated the nearby surfaces. The scent of cedar permeated the barn. Joe measured another plank and carried it to the table saw. His phone lit up, and he reached over to pause the music and answer the phone.

"This is Joe, what can I do for you?"

"Joe, it's Tara. You know that girl you were in the café with yesterday?"

He frowned slightly. Had Julie left something at the café? He didn't think so. She had stuffed everything in her backpack before they left. She hadn't taken him up on his offer to take her to Waterbury or Burlington either, but they'd had a nice lunch and he considered it progress. "Yeah, her name's Julie. Something wrong?"

"I think there is. Normally I'd mind my own business, but I saw her staring at her phone like the devil had just sent her a message and then she smashed it on the ground with a rock and threw it away. Joe, that girl's in trouble."

His hand clenched into a fist. "Where is she?"

"She turned around and headed back up Main Street."

"Toward the inn?"

"That would be my guess. She was in a hurry too."

"Thanks for calling."

"Sure thing, hon."

The line went dead, and Joe stared at the pile of woodchips under the saw. He barely knew Julie, but he wasn't able to ignore the fact she was clearly in trouble, fleeing from something or someone. He had no doubt she was preparing to do so again.

Striding out the side door of his barn where his workshop was located, he locked it behind him and pulled his truck keys from the front pocket of his jeans. He might be acting like a presumptuous fool, but he had to try to talk to her, see if he could help in any way. *Running from your troubles never helped anyone.*

He lived only a few minutes from the Monarch Inn, so the short drive didn't take him long. As he pulled into the parking lot, Julie jogged down the steps and over to a car. He pulled up behind her as she opened the car door and tossed her backpack inside. She glanced up and spotted his truck blocking in her car. A fleeting expression of alarm crossed her face before her gaze snagged his behind the wheel.

He lowered the window and smiled reassuringly. "Where you headed?"

Julie gazed around the parking lot. "It's time for me to go."

He sighed and draped his arm over the steering wheel, angling his head in her direction. "Tara from the café called me a little while ago. She was worried about you."

Her gaze swung back to his. "About me? Why?"

"She said you smashed your phone, threw it in the garbage, and you looked real upset."

Julie winced and folded her arms around her midriff.

"I happen to be a real good listener."

Her gaze darted to the ground.

"Let me help you, Julie."

"You don't even know me."

"Maybe not, but that doesn't mean I can't see you're in some kind of trouble and need a helping hand."

She gave him a sad smile. "You can't help me, Joe."

"How do you know? I might be a superhero in disguise."

A snort of laughter escaped her, and Julie's lips twitched. "Superhero, huh?"

"Okay, maybe not a superhero, but I'd still like to help you."

"The Boston police haven't been able to help me, but you think you can? I appreciate the offer, but there's nothing you can do."

"How do you know until you give me a chance? Tell me what's happening, Julie. At the very least I can listen. What's your other option? To keep running? Because it's obvious that's what you're doing."

Her brown eyes filled with tears, and she blinked them away and peered at the blue sky overhead.

"Come on. Get in the truck and tell me what's going on. We can go to my place, or go for a drive, or somewhere public if it makes you more comfortable."

Julie stared at the forest green truck and Joe behind the wheel. Was she crazy for even considering getting in the truck with him?

She was so darn tired.

Bending over, she grabbed her backpack off the passenger seat and locked her car. She walked around the front of his truck. He leaned over and pushed open the passenger door.

Climbing into the cab, she avoided his gaze. She shut the door, put on her seatbelt, and stared straight ahead.

"Where to?"

She shrugged. "It doesn't matter."

The truck rumbled forward. The inn disappeared from view as he drove out of the parking lot and onto the street. She hadn't checked out. She had just grabbed her things and ran. If he had tracked her by her credit card, then he might think she was still there when in fact she had left. He would only find her again if she used the card though. What could she possibly do?

What if it wasn't her card he tracked? What if he somehow

traced her phone? The phone now resided in the trash can, so that problem was solved. Oh God, what if he tracked her car?

"Julie are you okay?"

She stared out her window and blinked back the tears threatening to fall. "About six months ago, I started receiving pictures of myself taken in my apartment, in my car, out on the street, pretty much anywhere I frequented. I found them on my windshield, under my door, in my mail slot. I went to the police, but they basically said there's not much they can do. Two days ago, I was at work and pictures started flashing across my computer screen. I panicked and ran. I ended up here. I was walking through town and received a text message asking me what I was doing in Vermont and then telling me I couldn't run from him or her. I smashed the phone and threw it away, and you're right, I was going to run. What else can I do? The police haven't done anything."

"Do you know who sent the pictures and the text?"

Joe's fingers gripped the steering wheel. His jaw clenched, and his gaze narrowed. He was angry. On her behalf? The few friends she had told when it first started happening had shown interest and concern, but they hadn't been angry. They also hadn't stuck around when she started refusing to go out to restaurants or clubs out of fear.

He glanced at her as he pulled into a driveway. There was a white farmhouse with a wraparound porch and a giant red barn. A wooden sign hung above the large double doors proclaiming *Furniture by Joe* in gold lettering.

"I have no idea who is sending them."

"An ex-husband, boyfriend, someone you shot down?"

"As I told the police, I can't think of anyone. I've never been married, nor have I dated anyone for longer than a few months. It's never ended badly—it just ended. Nor have I spurned any guy asking me out on a date. I gave a list to the detectives of every guy I've ever dated or even those I remembered flirting with heavily. They checked them all out. Other than the couple of phone calls I got from previous boyfriends asking me what was going on because the police contacted them, nothing resulted from the questions."

"Who did you tell you were coming to Vermont?"

"Nobody. I left without even telling my boss I was leaving. I doubt I'll have a job to return to now. Besides, I didn't even know where I was going until I ended up here. I got in my car and drove with no destination in mind except to escape. I had to use a credit card at the inn. I kind of figured that's how he traced me, or by using my phone. I really don't want to contemplate it might be my car. That may be just the paranoia talking though."

"I don't think you're paranoid."

He put the truck in reverse and started backing up. Was he taking her back to the inn? Had he decided her troubles were too much baggage to deal with? She could hardly blame him. She was nothing to him.

Monarch Inn rose into view, and she sat forward ready to thank him for listening, but he didn't slow for the parking lot. "Where are you going?"

He spared her a swift glance. "The sheriff's."

"What?"

He pulled into a parking lot next to the town hall with its tall marble pillars. She spotted an SUV with *Sheriff*, emblazoned across the side.

"Laura Bennett is the sheriff. Tell her what you told me. This isn't Boston. Autumn Valley is a small town and, trust me, we don't take stalking lightly. She'll know what to do."

Julie gripped the arm rest on the door and stared at the dashboard. What possible good would telling the sheriff do? She wasn't planning to stick around Autumn Valley for her stalker to find her.

"You can't keep running. Talk to Sheriff Bennett. If you don't feel any differently afterwards...we'll discuss other options."

She raised an eyebrow and frowned. "Discuss?"

He winked at her and got out of the truck.

Sighing, she opened the door and hopped to the pavement. "I guess it can't do any harm."

Sheriff Bennett's calm, cinnamon-brown eyes and brisk, confident manner quickly put Julie at ease. She listened to her entire accounting, taking copious notes. Julie squirmed in her chair as the sheriff stared at her when she finished talking. "Which garbage can did you toss your phone into?"

"Umm...I'm not sure, by the grocery store, I think. Why?" Julie had peeled the paper from the plastic water bottle Joe had handed her earlier. She now crumbled the shredded pieces into a ball. Leaning forward, she chucked it into the garbage can next to the sheriff's desk.

"Because I want to see if the stalker was tracking your phone. I also want to take a peek at your car. Afterwards I'll call the Boston P.D. and see what they've got and update them." She stood, and Julie and Joe followed suit.

"I smashed the phone with a rock. I don't think you'll be able to get much information." Her cheeks heated, and she winced. She hadn't thought of getting evidence from her phone.

"You'd be surprised how indestructible phones can be. I'll be by the inn to let you know what I find and discuss a plan of action. In the meantime, don't go anywhere alone." She glanced at Joe.

He nodded at the sheriff.

Julie turned and met his gaze. "I'm not your responsibility."

Joe took ahold of her hand and ignored her comment. "Let's go back to the inn and have dinner. That should give Sheriff Bennett plenty of time to do what she needs to do."

Julie trailed behind him as he led her outside. The heat of his large hand engulfing hers and the tingle of awareness racing up her arm momentarily befuddled her brain.

Chapter Six

Ripples of indigo, tipped in white, spread out before her. The vast Lake Champlain, surrounded by hills of green, speckled with fall shades of yellow, orange, and red, perched on the border of Vermont and New York. Dozens of sailboats with bright rainbow-colored sails skimmed across the water. Julie smiled at the ducks bobbing along the current near the docks. The big white tour boat, *Spirit of Ethan Allen*, had just left with another group of tourists to view the lake.

"Are you sure you don't want to take a tour?" Joe leaned on the metal railing and gave her his heart melting grin accompanied by those adorable dimples.

"Not today." She surprised herself. Those words implied there would be another opportunity. Perhaps even another day trip with Joe. After they had gone to dinner the previous night, the sheriff had updated them on the investigation.

Her phone had been sent off to the lab to see if they could retrieve any data or determine how he had traced her. They had even searched her car, but thankfully hadn't found any tracking device. Sheriff Burke had talked to the Boston P.D. but they hadn't added much to her case. They did promise to check out her apartment and her place of employment after the latest round of photographs. For now, however, she was in limbo.

Joe had talked her into visiting the area today to take her mind off of everything. He hadn't needed to try all that hard. He made her feel safe, something she hadn't felt in a long time.

They had stopped in Waterbury and taken the required snapshots in the giant Ben & Jerry's ice cream lid and then continued to Burlington with the stipulation they would not be visiting his parents. He'd laughingly agreed to forgo the introduction this time.

"How about we meander up to Church Street? We should find a place or two for you to locate art supplies, and there are plenty of great places to grab a bite to eat for lunch."

"Sounds good."

He took her hand as they crossed the street and didn't let go on the other side of the intersection. She gazed at their joined hands. Was she crazy to spend time with him?

No, no more negative thoughts. Everyone was entitled to a day of freedom to enjoy themselves and not think of their troubles.

They wandered along the brick-lined thoroughfare of Church Street filled with an eclectic assortment of shops and restaurants. Its name derived from the prominent white church perched at the top of the street overlooking the bustling gathering location for the several colleges and universities that called Burlington home.

Julie found a delightful store which catered to local college students, and it carried a wide array of art supplies. She managed to restrain herself after a reminder she was on a tight budget, but she did purchase a small set of paints, brushes, and a few canvases.

The late September weather was warm enough to enjoy with only the occasional cool breeze ruffling her hair. She and Joe decided on a pub with outside seating for lunch. The black metal table and chairs were cool to the touch as she reclined against the seat back and crossed her legs. One of her favorite pastimes had always been people watching. It must be the artist within her who enjoyed observing the many differences and nuances of everyone she encountered.

The waiter took their order and delivered a glass of soda and one of water while Joe described some of the area attractions they could visit. He spoke as if she would be staying in the area long term.

A short, little, tan-colored dog with pointy ears trotted by. Its owner, a middle-aged woman with chin length blonde hair and large dark sunglasses, stopped to stare at her phone. The dog bounced around, despite being restrained by a leash—watching the people, bikes, and cars. A man with a huge, brown, Great Dane strolled around the corner. The little dog went on high alert. The man stopped to read a menu at one of the many restaurants with outdoor seating. The large dog plopped its butt down on the sidewalk and patiently waited for its owner to finish. The little dog pranced up behind the larger dog and started yipping away, bouncing a few steps away each time. It did this a few times, each time getting bolder and bolder until it stood inches from the large dog's tail. The Great Dane had ignored it until this point. It lazily pivoted its massive head and looked down at the nuisance yapping at its back. As soon as it did, the tiny dog leaped in the air and dashed back to its owner to hide behind her legs.

Julie laughed outright.

"That's a sight I'd like to see a lot more of."

She glanced over at him with a wide smile. "The dog?"

"No, your laughter."

Her cheeks heated. "Oh." It had been awhile since she'd had anything to laugh about.

"So, why Boston? Did you grow up there?"

"No, but I attended college there and fell in love with the city, so when I got offered a job after graduation I jumped at the opportunity. And I've been in Boston ever since."

She had borrowed Joe's phone yesterday to call and talk to her boss. And to explain her abrupt departure and to warn him the police department intended to stop by to check her workstation. Her boss had been sympathetic but had warned Julie, her job would not be held indefinitely. Her vacation time would be used and once depleted he expected her to return.

The idea of returning to her apartment or even her workplace caused her muscles to tense up.

More choices she had to make. But not today. Today was for carefree fun. Worrying and decisions needed to wait. At some point she would have to return to Boston, but could she go back to living in her apartment knowing the stalker had been there and taken photos of her unaware? Would moving to a different, more secure apartment change anything?

The waiter returned with her order of ziti with chicken and pesto along with Joe's order of a pulled pork sandwich and chips. Basil and parmesan combined to create a delightful aroma. Joe took a bite of his sandwich. Drops of sauce and pork splattered on his plate from the messy concoction. He managed to juggle the sandwich and his napkin as he took another bite. A smile teased her lips when she sampled the pasta. The pesto was a bit strong for her tastes, but still pleasing.

"Were you an artist prodigy or did you find your talent later in college?"

"I certainly wouldn't call myself a prodigy, but I've been drawing since as far back as I can remember. My teachers always encouraged me. I felt special when they offered praise or hung up one of my drawings on the blackboard. Once I was in high school, I took every art class they offered. It was where I was the happiest."

***

Joe noticed she didn't mention her parents offering her any praise, and he wanted to hug her. She wasn't ready for closer contact, however. His family were affectionate people, always hugging, or even just a casual touch of comfort or love. Julie stiffened whenever he took her hand, but then relaxed. She didn't pull away, and he took it as a good sign.

She tucked her loose hair behind her ear, the blue ends brushing against her slim neck, and twirled her fork around on her plate. Her pasta dish long forgotten as her gaze wandered around the area. Her eyes lit up occasionally, and a smile quirked the corner of her mouth as she studied the people milling the promenade.

Not a hint of makeup adorned her skin, and she didn't need a drop. Every time he looked at her, she got prettier.

Her agreement to spend the day with him had come as a pleasant shock. He had been sure she would refuse. He'd kept the conversation light on purpose to take away a little of the sadness lurking in her eyes.

Joe took a sip of the tepid water and folded his hands together over his abdomen, content to watch her enjoying the afternoon. Perhaps she'd enjoy a stroll around the city, or a movie—anything to prolong the time he could spend in her company.

Chapter Seven

Julie trudged up the inn stairs to her room. She'd spent the day painting the faded red covered bridge at the edge of town. Satisfaction battled with exhaustion. A nap sounded appealing. Collapsing on her bed for an hour or so before she had to think of a solution for dinner seemed the perfect way to end the afternoon. Her cash supply was dwindling. She had stockpiled a small supply of snacks in her room to negate the need to eat out, but even that stash was rapidly depleting. She'd lost enough weight over the past six months from fear and worry so her clothes were already loose on her. She really couldn't afford to lose much more. A predicament her high school self would have envied.

What was Joe doing right now? She hadn't seen him since their trip to Burlington two days ago. Her nose wrinkled as she realized she missed his easy smile and the quiet way he had about him. He made her feel hopeful everything would be okay. He'd told her he had deliveries to make yesterday. He'd finished a few furniture pieces and needed to deliver them to his clients, so she wouldn't see him then, but at the back of her mind she had expected him to drop by today.

She hesitated on the top tread of the stairs and then shook her head at her musings. Even if he had, she wouldn't have known. She'd been gone the entire day, and she had no phone for him to call. She supposed she could check at the front desk to see if he had left a message, but then she'd feel silly, and if she was honest with herself, disappointed if he hadn't. There had been a couple checking in when she had arrived and therefore Conner, the person behind the desk, was busy. But maybe she would wander back downstairs in a bit. If a message had been left, she was sure he'd wave her over or something. It was a small inn, not a huge city hotel with thousands of guests after all. She wasn't an anonymous, invisible person lost in the throng of the crowd here. Something she needed to get accustomed to.

The hair on her arms raised. A blast of frigid air surrounded her. Julie whirled around, looking in every direction. *What on Earth?*

No one was present in the hall. The murmur of voices drifted up the stairs. It must have been the air conditioning turning on. She peered up at the ceiling to see if she was standing under a vent. Smiling slightly, she stepped forward to go to her room.

Her heart clenched in her chest. Her throat constricted as her mouth opened and a small puff of air released. A tiny white cloud of breath hung in the frigid air but that wasn't what held her paralyzed.

A woman stood in front of her door.

A transparent woman.

The apparition raised its arm and opened its mouth.

Julie spun around and fled. Adrenalin pumping through her system, she raced down the stairs and barreled into a large, immovable object.

A scream bubbled up inside her throat but she choked it back.

"Easy there, Julie. What's the rush?"

She blinked up at a smiling Joe. His arms held her steady, but his smile slowly faded. "Julie? What's wrong?" He gripped her shoulders.

"I...there." She swallowed and tried again. "There was a woman."

"A woman?" He looked up the stairs. "What woman? Did she say something to upset you? Do something?"

"No, no, she was a..."

He stared at her patiently, a worried frown on his face.

Rubbing the bridge of her nose, her gaze dropped to the floor. "You're probably going to think I'm crazy, but there was a ghost standing in front of the door to my room."

Silence radiated above her.

She raised her head and shrugged her shoulders. "I'm not crazy."

His mouth quirked, and he tugged her resistant body against him for a hug.

She stood stiffly in his arms but didn't attempt to step away. Her nerves were still on edge from her ghostly encounter, and she liked having him hold her.

"I know what I saw," she mumbled against his green plaid shirt.

"I believe you. You're the first I've heard that's seen her. Usually, people just hear her laughing."

"What?"

Julie canted her head to the side. "You mean you believe there is a ghost here? Other people know about this?"

"Sure, don't most old buildings have tales of a ghost or two? At least the inn's is a happy woman."

"She didn't look terribly happy when I saw her."

"What do you mean?"

"She looked upset, agitated. She waved her arm and opened her mouth, and I wasn't waiting around to hear what she might say. She wasn't laughing, that's for sure."

Joe frowned and glanced up the stairs again. "Why don't you go have a seat and I'll go upstairs and have a look around, okay?"

Julie glanced at the inviting armchair he indicated with a jerk of his chin. "Suit yourself. I have no intention of searching out a ghost in order to have a conversation." She meandered over toward the chair while Joe climbed the stairs two at a time.

Before she plopped into the chair her conscience got the better of her. What was she letting him wander into? What if the ghost was angry and dangerous? Could a ghost hurt someone?

Sighing, Julie followed him up the stairs at a much slower pace. Leave it to her to see an angry ghost instead of the laughing one everyone else encountered.

She peeked around the top of the stairs. Joe strode down the hall toward her.

"I haven't seen or heard anything. Guess she left."

Gazing at her door where the ghost had stood, Julie grimaced.

"Give me your key and I'll check out your room."

Handing over the key, she trailed behind him. She had to get past the fear churning in her stomach. Otherwise how was she going to stay here at the inn, let alone sleep here?

Joe glanced over his shoulder. "You want to wait over in the sitting area?"

"Alone? I don't think so."

He smiled and opened the door.

Drawers hung open or upside down on the rug. A glance in the bathroom showed her toiletries piled in the sink. The floral scent of the inn's body lotion she had applied to her skin just this morning filled the air. An open bottle rested on its side on the tile floor, making a small puddle of creamy white.

"Julie, go downstairs and tell Conner to call Sheriff Bennett."

She stared at the back of Joe's head as he stood in front of her, blocking her view of the rest of the room. "What am I supposed to tell him? The resident ghost doesn't like me and threw a temper tantrum in my room?" There was no way she would ever be able to sleep here again.

"It wasn't a ghost."

"What?"

He grasped her shoulders. "Someone vandalized your room." He glanced over her shoulder to the hallway behind her. "In fact, we should both go downstairs. We shouldn't touch anything, and I don't want you to be alone."

She shifted to glance around him, but he blocked her. "Let's go downstairs."

A cold sweat engulfed her skin. Her arm jerked as she held her open hand over the squeezing pain in her chest.

"The stalker's found me, haven't they?"

Chapter Eight

Julie pushed past Joe to see what he had been trying to hide from her. Stripped bedding lay dumped in a pile on the floor. A handful of photographs lay scattered over the bed. The photos were all head shots of Julie. Garish red slashes criss-crossed her face in each picture.

"Julie." Joe touched her shoulder. She flinched, stepped away, and wrapped her arms around her waist.

Part of her wished she'd let him continue to block her view.

Her stalker was here.

Where could she run to now?

The soft murmur of voices registered behind her. Joe was on the phone to the sheriff. Her gaze remained glued to the black and white eight by ten photographs. She couldn't look away. A tremor shook her.

There was nowhere to hide. He or she would find her wherever she went.

Joe stepped in front of her, shielding her view, and took her shoulders in his hands. His movements and face were a blur. She blinked, trying to focus. His mouth opened, but she only heard a loud buzzing in her ears. The edges of her vision blackened, and the lure of unconscious oblivion tugged at her.

"Julie!"

Joe yanked her up into his arms and strode out of the room, into the hallway, and over to the sitting area.

The movement snapped her back into focus. She grasped the soft material of his flannel shirt in her fists. She should protest him carrying her. She wasn't a child, she was a grown woman, and she shouldn't need to lean on anyone.

But it felt so good. The strength of his arms and warmth from his body surrounded her. Just for a moment, she would allow herself this comfort.

"I'm all right. Put me down."

He sat in one of the chairs with her cradled in his arms. "There, we're down."

A reddish hue darkened his cheekbones. His nostrils flared. The laughter usually dancing in his eyes was absent for the moment. His dimples had gone into hiding as well. She rested her head against his shoulder and breathed deeply of the fresh cut wood scent which always lingered around him.

Joe wrapped his arms tighter around her and kissed the top of her head. Tears filled her eyes, but she willed them away and blinked until the moisture dissipated.

"Sheriff Bennett will be here any minute."

She knew Joe meant well, but she didn't hold the same confidence in law enforcement's capabilities. Six months of terrorizing and the Boston police had come up empty. What hope could she have that Vermont law enforcement would accomplish what their neighboring state hadn't?

A tall, slender man with chestnut colored hair jogged up the stairs. His piercing green gaze landed on her and Joe. He nodded in their direction, she felt Joe return the nod, as the man walked to her room and scanned the interior from the doorway. He mumbled an expletive before he switched direction and approached them. "Miss

Roy, I'm Kyle Palmer, the owner of the inn. Can I do anything for you? Get you anything?"

Julie shook her head. "No. Thank you."

"Kyle, do you have any information?"

"No. Right after you texted me telling me what happened, Sheriff Bennett called and instructed me not to let anyone in the room or go traipsing around outside destroying potential evidence. She said the state police have been called in since a major crime has been committed. They will be in charge of the investigation." He glanced at her before returning his gaze to Joe. "I did walk through the inn to see if anything else was ...amiss. Nothing is. I informed Conner at the front desk. He hasn't seen anyone other than our current guests and those dining in the Café. They're all accounted for."

The top of Sheriff Bennett's brown head appeared in the stairwell. Her calm brown gaze surveyed everyone and everything. After examining Julie's room, she walked over and crouched in front of Julie.

"I need you to walk me through exactly what happened, step by step." She glanced at Joe. "I only want to hear from Julie. You told me what you saw, now I need to hear her accounting."

Julie winced. She'd been through this before. At least she didn't have to do it in the middle of the cacophony of the Boston police station. And thankfully, she wasn't alone this time either. Joe's strong presence was a balm to her cracked and tarnished armor.

She gave her statement, from her arrival at the inn, the ghost's serendipitous appearance, Joe's arrival, and then the discovery of the vandalism. Other than a quick widening of the eyes, the sheriff made no comment regarding the ghostly visitor. Julie had momentarily wondered if she should avoid mentioning the apparition, but it had happened, and if it made her sound like a crazy person so be it. She was too weary to care anymore.

When the state police arrived, the Sheriff stepped aside to talk to them. They too disappeared into her room.

The inn owner stepped closer to her and Joe. "Describe the woman."

She stared at the man trying to ascertain whether he believed she was crazy or not. All she perceived on his face was curiosity.

Sighing, she rested against Joe's wide chest. Julie supposed she should have climbed off his lap and sat in one of the other chairs, but she couldn't dredge up the will to move. And Joe didn't seem inclined to let her go.

"Other than transparent I'm not really sure what to say. She scared the hell out of me, and I ran." She concentrated on the image in her head of the woman standing in front of her door. "She was wearing a dress, old-fashioned. I'm sorry, but that's all I can tell you."

He nodded. "It's the start of the fall foliage season so I don't have another room available for you. I imagine it will be a while before the police are finished with your room. Would you care to have dinner in the Café while you wait? On the house, of course."

Stiffening, her gaze shot to the doorway of her room. Could she go back in there? Did she have a choice?

"Julie will be staying with me."

Staring at Joe, she opened her mouth to refuse. The owner leaned toward them. "Perhaps that is for the best." She didn't blame him for not wanting her to remain a guest at the inn. Her presence had caused damage to his property and possibly endangered his other guests. "I believe it best if we kept that information private. Tell no one but Sheriff Bennett where Miss Roy will be staying. If anyone inquires, I'll be sure my staff informs them she left town." "Thank you, Kyle." Joe nodded.

"Miss Roy, if there is anything I can do to help you, please don't hesitate to ask."

Tears threatened at the back of her eyes once again, and she swallowed hard and forced a smile. "Thank you."

He gave her a slight bow before turning and leaving.

Joe glanced down. "Thank you for not arguing."

"I can't stay with you."

"Why not?"

"Because we barely know each other. You can't just invite a stranger to stay with you. Especially one with a crazy stalker." A shudder slid through her.

"You're not a stranger, and that's even more reason for you to stay with me. You need help. Let me help you, please."

She should be saying no, but the words weren't coming. She had nowhere else to go. Julie didn't want to keep running. She stared at his kind face patiently waiting for a response.

"You can stay in the house. I have a small studio apartment in the barn for the days I'm too lazy to walk back to the house. I'll sleep there. All completely aboveboard."

Did it make her a bad person to say yes? Did it make her weak?

"Oh, I also bought you a cell phone. It's a prepaid one you don't have to worry someone can trace. I was bringing it by tonight when you came running down the stairs." He shrugged. "Well, that and I was going to convince you to have dinner with me." He winked at her and one of his dimples popped out.

A flutter started in her abdomen. He'd bought her a phone, an untraceable one.

"Have I told you about Max?"

"Max?"

"My dog. He's a German Shepherd, looks a bit ferocious, but he's really a big baby. He's great at alerting me when anyone comes on the property though. Barks like it's Armageddon. I've got a cat too, Lucy. She came with the place and mostly stays in the barn. Although considering she's expecting kittens, she must have left the barn to do a bit of wandering."

"Kittens?"

"Mm-hmm...surprised the heck out of me when I brought her to the vet. I thought she was just getting a little chubby."

Julie chewed on her bottom lip. He'd bought her a phone, and he had a dog and soon-to-be kittens.

"There's a deer and two fawns on the property who like to pay a visit to my yard every now and again. A bunch of turkeys too."

A smile twitched at her lips.

Joe noticed the movement and the hot knot of rage which had fisted in his chest at the site of the destruction done to her room and belongings eased a little. There wasn't a single instance in his entire life when he had been so angry. In that moment he'd realized he was capable of violence. To defend those he cared for he could and would use anything and everything at his disposal.

And Julie was someone he cared for, deeply.

He had no explanation for his feelings, maybe there was none. His father liked to tell the story of the first time he laid eyes on Joe's mother. He'd known she was the one for him. She had been waitressing in her parents' Italian restaurant, and when she walked up to his father's table, he claimed he lost the power of speech. His mother always laughed when he told this story and added, "There was this handsome stranger sitting there, gaping at me. I thought I had sauce on my face or something. I was about to run to the backroom to check my face in the mirror when suddenly he proposes to me out of the blue!" His dad would simply reply, "The heart always knows."

It might be that simple. He couldn't say. What he did know was he would do everything within his power to protect Julie and keep her safe. He wanted to take the fear out of her eyes.

"Say yes, at least for tonight." If he could get her to agree to tonight, he'd worry about getting her to stay longer tomorrow.

Chapter Nine

"Here's the linen closet. If you need any towels, they're here."

Julie gave Joe a perfunctory nod as he showed her around the upstairs of his house. He pointed out the bathroom and bedrooms. He had already placed her meager belongings in the spare room earlier before he'd cooked her a dish of pasta for dinner. Luckily, all the possessions she had brought with her were still in her backpack, which she kept with her at all times, so nothing had to be left at the inn as part of the crime scene. It's not like she would have wanted anything her stalker might have touched, anyway.

Max sauntered by and plopped down on the blue and white throw rug next to the bed in the guestroom. Joe had introduced them when they arrived, and Max had presented her with his big paw to shake. He'd leaned against her earlier, and she'd dug her fingers into his thick black and tan coat.

"That's the tour. Anything I can get you before I head over to the barn?"

Tension seeped throughout Julie's bones. She folded her arms around her abdomen and stared through the doorway into the bedroom.

"Do you think you could stay for a little while? I'm not ready to be alone yet."

"Of course, I'll stay as long as you need me to." He tucked a lock of her hair behind her ear. "Would you like to go back downstairs and watch television for a while? I think I can drum up some popcorn."

"That would be nice. Thank you, for everything."

"It's my pleasure." He clasped her hand in his and tugged her toward and then down the stairs. She settled into a corner of the brown couch with a bright yellow throw pillow in her lap, while Joe stood in front of the television with the remote, scrolling through the channels.

"How about a comedy?"

"Sounds perfect. I could use a laugh."

"He set the remote on the table. Do you want me to make popcorn?"

She lightly shook her head. "I'm not hungry."

"Popcorn isn't for hunger."

"Oh? What's it for then?"

"T.V. accompaniment."

Julie smiled. "Well then, be my guest, but I'm fine without it."

He sat on the couch next to her, draped an arm over her shoulders, and pulled her against his side.

She didn't resist. Instead, she snuggled against him and laid her head on his shoulder. "No popcorn?"

"Nah, we'll save it for another time."

The sitcom elicited a chuckle or two from each of them before it ended, and another took its place. Her eyes grew heavy, and her thoughts drifted.

Joe watched Julie's eyes slide shut, and her body settled into sleep. The dark crescents under her lashes caused a frown to twitch at his mouth. He slouched farther into the couch, and gently angled her, so she had more room and rested comfortably while he watched over her.

Julie reminded him a bit of Scrappy, a dog he'd had when he was a kid. His family had visited an animal shelter, and Joe insisted on bringing home a mongrel of a dog no one else had wanted. Not because of its looks, which were homely at best, but because it growled, yipped, or cowered if anyone got too close. After much pleading and bargaining, his parents had reluctantly agreed to bring the dog home for a trial period. With instructions from the woman at the shelter, the vet, and several pet manuals, Joe had patiently coaxed the dog he named Scrappy into trusting him.

Skittish and primed to attack if cornered, Julie embodied the little dog's spirit. She'd been through a lot, but she wasn't defeated. Letting someone help her appeared to be a foreign concept to the woman, which made him think she didn't have people in her life she could rely on.

Joe's patience had gifted him with a playful companion in Scrappy for almost ten years. Would patience be enough to convince Julie to stay and let him help her? Or would he wake up one morning to find her gone?

"It looks like the perp entered and exited using the side porch. No one reported seeing anyone. The state police collected several fingerprints, and they will be combing through them and eliminating the inn employees. I'll need a set of yours too for matching."

Julie nodded absently. Once again, her stalker had slipped away with no one the wiser after delivering devastation to her life.

Sheriff Bennett shifted on the wooden chair where she sat opposite Julie. Joe stood, leaning against the kitchen sink with his arms folded across his chest. The sheriff had arrived shortly after a pancake breakfast Joe had made once she'd wakened on the couch in the living room. Disorientation and fear shrouded her at first, but then Joe had sauntered in from the kitchen with wet hair and sipping at a steaming cup of coffee, and the tension had melted away. She'd clutched the quilt he must have covered her with at some point and returned his smile.

"Julie, they found a tracer in your phone tucked into the back with the battery. That's how he or she knew where you were."

A numbness settled over her. She'd known she was being tracked somehow, but how had the tracker gotten into her phone? It meant someone had been close to her and managed to slip it in without her noticing. She always kept her cellphone with her, like most people in this day and age. At least she had before she smashed it with a rock. When and how had they managed?

"I think it's a good idea for you to keep a low profile until we catch this creep. Stay here at Joe's and let him think you've moved on. Park your car out of sight behind the barn. Meanwhile we'll be keeping a watch out. Folks tend to notice strangers around here. Sure, we get the leaf peepers this time of year, but nonresidents stick out like a sore thumb."

"I wasn't planning on staying here."

The sheriff glanced at Joe.

"You heard the sheriff, it's best if you stay here. Stop running. Don't let him take any more from you. Let me help you. Let us help you."

Julie cradled the mug of coffee in her hands and stared down at the dark brew. It warmed her chilled hands, and the rich aroma filled her nostrils. "I don't understand why any of you encourage me to stay. I would think you'd want me and whatever danger stalking me as far away as possible."

The sheriff smiled. "That's the beauty of small towns. We take care of our own."

"But I'm not one of your own. I'm from Boston."

She stood and pushed the chair in. "You're one of our own by association." She glanced at Joe with a smirk. "And we don't take kindly when they are messed with."

Julie gazed at Joe, who blinked innocently at her and then winked. She rolled her eyes. Was everyone crazy? Or was she the crazy one? Did normal people behave this way? It wasn't like she was exactly experienced in the area of what normal people did or didn't do.

"That's my cue to leave. Call me if anything changes. I'll notify you when I get any updates on the case."

Julie thanked the sheriff but remained sitting at the table while Joe walked her out. Max trotted over to sit next to her and placed his head in her lap with a small whine. She ruffled his fur.

"What do you think, boy? Should I stay or go?"

"Max and I have a unique communication, and I can tell you he definitely thinks you should stay."

She glanced up at Joe standing in the doorway.

"He does, does he?"

"Without a doubt. Just look at him. That's him pleading with you to stay."

Max's brown eyes peered up at her, and she laughed.

"Who am I to argue with such an adorable guy?"

At the moment, she wasn't certain if she meant the canine or Joe.

Chapter Ten

Fingers streaked with a rainbow of shades—green, splashes of yellow and orange, and a few dots of blue — Julie rubbed the tip of her nose with the back of her wrist. She was trying to capture the meandering brook edged with moss-covered rocks at the base of a copse of trees covered in leaves. Leaves beginning to change color before they would eventually fall to the ground. Her canvas and easel perched on Joe's back lawn. She had chosen to work with oils today because of the ease of blending the colors to achieve her desired result, and by working outside, no one would be bothered with the smell of the solvents. Not that Joe was likely to complain. He didn't grumble about anything as far as she could tell.

One day Joe came home from grocery shopping with a large bag full of more canvases and a new sketchpad—claiming he wanted her to paint some landscapes of his property. Even though she guessed he worded it in such a way, she would be less likely to refuse his gift, Julie had accepted with a heartfelt thank you, having already filled the canvases she had purchased, and her fingers still itched to paint more.

She'd been in his home a couple of weeks and his calm, easygoing demeanor never faltered. They'd fallen into a bit of a pattern or routine. Preparing breakfast for the two of them was her job, something she had insisted on because she may not be the best cook, but she wanted to do her share. Joe on the other hand could really cook so dinner was his department. She teased him by calling him a chef in another life. He replied it was his Italian upbringing and the fact his grandparents had owned and run a restaurant for years.

Thankfully, during this time no more stalker incidents had occurred. Good news, of course, wonderful really, but there hadn't been any breaks or updates on the case either. It was like the stalker had just popped in to wreak havoc in her life and remind her of their presence and then disappeared into thin air once again—making it impossible for the police to have a clue as to who or where they were. Perhaps the stalker was a ghost like the woman at the Monarch Inn.

She paused and lifted the paintbrush from the canvas. That was a terrifying thought. Could ghosts stalk someone? She gave herself a hard shake and resumed painting the sky, adding a stray puffy cloud of white that drifted into view above. Dire thoughts would not mar such a beautiful day. Besides, she'd heard of poltergeists moving objects, but she'd certainly never heard of a ghost or specter taking pictures of someone.

A chuckle reverberated in her throat.

"What's so funny?"

Turning her head, she smiled at Joe as he stopped next to her and examined her painting.

"You are amazingly gifted. You know that, don't you?"

Bumping his shoulder with her own, she looked back at the canvas.

"I mean it. I'm in awe of what you can create."

The heat of a blush stung her cheeks. "Nature did the hard work. I'm just trying my best to capture a piece of its beauty."

"You're too modest. You should be proud of what you can do."

"Sounds a little like the pot calling the kettle black. I seem to remember you changing the subject rather abruptly when you showed me your workshop in the barn the other day and I compli-mented you on the beautiful pieces of furniture you've created."

Joe shrugged. "That's different. You create this practically out of air with just some drops of colored paint. The wood I use is the beauty. I only try to show it in its best light."

Shaking her head, she took his hand in hers. "No, it's these hands that manage to bring out the beauty in the wood by creating some-thing brand new and magical which only your eyes can see the poten-tial of when you view the wood in its natural state. Everyone else would simply see a tree, an exceptionally nice tree perhaps, but still a tree."

Joe lifted their joined hands and kissed the back of hers. Warmth spread through Julie, and she got a little hitch in her chest.

"Let's make a deal. We'll both do better at accepting a compli-ment about our work, okay?"

Julie nodded. "Deal."

Max, who had been lying in the sun a few feet away, let out a short bark and wagged his tail.

"See, even Max agrees." Joe grinned and draped an arm around her shoulders to hug her. He placed a swift kiss on the top of her head.

Some people were just born huggers. She was not, nor was she raised in a demonstrative family. Affection was reserved for holidays, and then it was a perfunctory peck on the cheek. Joe, on the other hand, was always holding her hand, giving her a quick hug, an occa-sional kiss on the head. She gathered from the stories he told about his family and growing up they were an affectionate, close bunch. She never thought she would do well with someone like that, but she found herself liking it more and more. In fact, she found herself hoping for more altogether. Wasn't that a kick in the pants?

Amid the turmoil, undecided mess of her life, she, the one who avoided romantic entanglements and who was *Miss keep it light and friendly*, wanted to know what it was like to really kiss Joe.

"What's that look for?"

"Hmm...what?"

"You got quiet and your eyes got kind of squinty, and these tiny little lines appeared right there." He gently tapped the spot between her eyebrows.

"Oh."

"Oh? What's going on in that pretty head of yours?"

"Why haven't you kissed me? I mean really kissed me. Has the debacle of my life erased your interest? I mean I get it if it does. How could it not? It's—"

"Julie!"

She blinked owlishly up at him as he cupped her face in his hands. "What?"

"I haven't lost interest by a long shot. I was trying not to pressure you or frankly, scare you off."

"Oh," she repeated dully.

He chuckled, and his mouth spread into a grin. Those darn, irresistible dimples smirked.

Joe dipped his head, and his chocolate brown eyes gazed into Julie's, and she found herself holding her breath. Anticipating it like it was her first kiss.

His full lips caressed hers tentatively. His warm breath mingled with hers when she finally released it on a sigh.

His hands cradled her head while his fingers delved into her hair. He had a working man's hands. They weren't smooth or soft. They were hard, yet incredibly gentle. Callused, yet tender and oh, so strong.

She raised her own hands to cover his.

Pausing infinitesimally, his gaze devoured her features before his lips captured hers in a deeper kiss.

Her eyes drifted closed as she lost herself in the pleasure of his touch.

A sharp bark caused her to jump away, ending the kiss.

Max sat at their feet with his head cocked to the side. He lifted a leg and pawed at the air in front of him.

"Get your own girl, pal."

She laughed and looked up at Joe. He pressed a lingering kiss to her lips and whispered, "Do you still doubt my interest? Because I'm more than happy to continue convincing you. We could move the discussion inside away from the jealous dog."

Julie dropped her head to his chest. "I shouldn't have started this. I'm a bad bet. I'm terrible at relationships."

"Says who?"

"Says my history. I don't know how to do this. I will screw it up, and I have no business starting something with you when my life is so messed up."

"First of all, you can't plan feelings. They happen when they do and with whom they want. Second of all..." He lifted her chin from his chest. "Julie, look at me."

Raising her gaze, she nibbled on her lip.

"Second of all, no one is keeping score. Your past and your relationships don't matter. Right here and now it's just the two of us. We can't predict the future. I, for one, can't wait to see where it goes, and I fully plan to enjoy every step of the way."

Chapter Eleven

The rain cascaded down, forming puddles and covering everything in a wet sheen. Drops of water lined up underneath the balcony railing waiting their turn to plummet to the deck. A steady drip from the gutters could be heard over the pitter patter of rain. Joe leaned against the sliding door to the balcony attached to his apartment and gazed out over his backyard.

He'd spent the morning cutting the panels and strips of oak and mahogany he planned to piece together to make a dining room table for a client. He'd come upstairs to the studio apartment for a quick shower to wash away the sawdust coating his skin. He had planned to put another coat of stain on a set of chairs, but the rain had captured his attention, and his mind wandered in directions other than work. Like to a certain pretty little brunette with the ends of her hair dyed blue.

The kiss they had shared the day before had scorched his insides and left him wanting more, but the last thing he wanted to do was to rush her.

Determination to let her call the shots made him proceed slowly with albeit minor guidance from him prodding her in the right direction. She'd surprised and delighted him with the question about his interest waning. It meant she had feelings for him, or at least she was thinking of him romantically. Had he been too subtle with his attention while trying not to scare her away by overwhelming her and declaring his feelings so soon? No problem there. He was more than happy to kick it up a notch.

Pulling the green T-shirt over his head, he wondered if there were any signals from Julie he might have missed and vowed to be more diligent at observing her for any clues to her feelings, so he knew which way to proceed. He had a single goal in mind, to make sure she gave their relationship a chance.

Make it two goals—keeping her safe as well.

With one last glimpse out the glass, Joe left the apartment. It occurred to him the rain was keeping Julie inside. Perhaps she was sketching or painting in the house, and maybe she wouldn't mind a little company.

Julie folded the last of the towels and carried them upstairs to the linen closet. Although Joe insisted she not do the laundry, he wanted her to be a guest, she needed to feel like she was pulling her weight even if it was only by doing the household tasks. He wouldn't hear of her paying any rent. She had tried to write him a check. She was afraid to access her bank account for fear of tipping off the stalker somehow, but if she wrote him a check, he could cash it once this mess cleared up. He refused however, got rather stiff-necked and changed the subject.

They needed to come to an understanding that worked for both of them. She didn't want or need to feel indebted to Joe. It put whatever possible relationship they might have on shaky ground.

The sound of the kitchen door opening and closing echoed up the stairs as she started down them.

"Julie?"

Joe appeared around the corner into the living room just as she reached the bottom of the stairs. She smiled at him. "Hello, did you come in for lunch?"

"No, not exactly. Although it is a good idea. I came in to see if you were free. How about a picnic lunch?" Julie glanced out the window at the rain.

Joe chuckled. "Not outside. We can have an indoor picnic, move the furniture around, spread out a blanket. What do you say?"

"I've never had an indoor picnic. Come to think of it, I don't recall ever having an outdoor one either."

"Perfect. You can have your first one with me."

"Okay, what are we going to have on this picnic?"

"Leave that to me. In fact, leave everything to me. You sit down and relax and just give me a few minutes to pull it all together."

Sighing, she wandered over to stand in front of him. "Joe, we need to talk."

"That doesn't send any warm fuzzy feelings my way. What's wrong? You don't want a picnic after all?"

"No, that's not it. I want to talk about you not wanting me to do my share. It's important to me."

"Okay, you want to help prepare the picnic?"

"No, I mean yes, that's a good start. I need to feel like we are on equal footing, or at least as much as possible. I want you to let me write you a check for rent. Even though you can't cash it yet, it still acts as a legal instrument or contract or whatever stating I owe you the money."

Joe sighed roughly and ran his fingers through his damp, curly hair. He stared intently at the floor before meeting her gaze. "If it's that important to you, then fine, I'll take the check."

A smile bloomed over her face and a weight lifted off her shoulders. "Really? Thank you. I'll get my checkbook right now."

"Julie, geez, can't it wait a little while? Let's have our picnic. Who knew accepting money from a woman would make her so happy?"

"Fine, but you will have the check by the end of the day. It's important for me not to feel so beholden to you or anyone. Please don't misunderstand or believe I'm not eternally grateful to you for everything you've done. I feel that two people who are becoming involved with one another should be on equal footing. That's all."

"Why? Isn't a relationship about people supporting one another with their strengths and complementing each other? No two individuals are ever going to be exactly equal in any category, are they? I mean, all the relationships I know, my parents, siblings, aunts, uncles, and on down the list, thrive because one part of the couple balances out the other one. We each have our strengths and weaknesses, no matter what they are, whether it be money, cooking, emotional support, knowledge, or whatever."

Julie stared at his earnest expression. What he described sounded rather ideal and improbable, at least in her experience. He cited his family as a guide. Her family consisted of her parents, hardly ideal. One of their common themes during arguments when she was a child was who did what, bottom line who did more. No surprise she didn't like to feel indebted to anyone.

"We've had two very different upbringings and examples. How about I promise to not see everything as a balance of scales, and you let me attempt to feel like I'm pulling my weight?"

Joe slipped his arm around her waist and pulled her against him. "I can do that. As long as you understand my inherent desire to cherish you and take care of you any way I can won't go away. I'll try not to be too overbearing."

Resting her palms against his chest, she smiled. "I'm not opposed to the cherishing. I just need to feel equal."

His hands massaged her back in a languorous movement. "Feel free to cherish me equally. In fact, I believe we could go upstairs and cherish one another right now."

She linked her hands behind his neck and smiled. "Oh, you do, do you?"

"Most definitely."

He captured her lips in an ardent kiss. Their desire rose, and she arched against his strong body as he embraced her completely.

The pealing of the doorbell broke through the haze of lust. She pulled back from his kiss to see Joe glare over her shoulder.

"Next time I get you in my arms I'm going to make sure there are no possible interruptions."

Julie chuckled and glanced over her shoulder to see the outline of two people at the front door through the frosted glass.

"Who are they?"

Joe sighed. "My parents."

Chapter Twelve

His parents? Julie dropped her hands and stepped back out of Joe's arms. Her gaze strayed to the stairs. "I'll go up to my room while you visit with them."

Joe snagged her hand as she turned away. "They won't bite, promise."

He tugged her toward the door.

Her gaze ping ponged between the door and the stairs, getting farther and farther away. She could wrench her hand free and disappear into her bedroom. Joe wouldn't argue too strenuously. It wasn't in his nature. Yet, he clearly wanted to introduce her, and he had done so much for her. How bad could meeting his parents be? She'd never met the parents of any guy she dated before. Her relationships had never progressed that far. It would have been a hard no for her if they had.

Meeting someone's parents meant long-term commitment in her mind, not something she ever felt ready for in any relationship she'd been in. She had nothing against a monogamous committed relationship, but it wasn't something she coveted or even thought she might want some day. Both required trust. Trust in the other person and trust in yourself to make the right choices.

The door loomed in front of them. Biting her lip, she took a deep fortifying breath. Joe winked at her over his shoulder before opening the door and greeting his parents. "Hi, Mom, Dad. To what do I owe this surprise visit?"

Joe's dad was an inch or two shorter than him, had a receding hairline, and the same twinkling brown eyes. His mom was petite. Dark hair pulled back into a bun with a curl or two escaping to cascade down and rest against her cheek. Wide brown eyes gazed at Julie with reserved curiosity. Her gaze drifted lower and paused over their joined hands.

"Well now, who is this pretty young lady?"

Joe kissed his mom on the cheek and clapped his dad on the shoulder as they stepped into the house. "This is Julie Roy."

She pulled her hand free to shake both of theirs and smiled at them. "It's nice to meet you both."

"You see, Adriane, I told you there was a perfectly good reason our son has been too preoccupied of late to visit with his family."

Julie stiffened. She'd been keeping him from his family?

"Dad...I saw everyone for Sunday dinner." Joe ushered them into the living room while she tucked both her hands in the front pockets of her capris and stood behind the couch. Joe had gone to his parents' house every Sunday since she moved in. He had asked her to go each time, but she had declined. He hadn't pushed too hard because they both believed it would be best for Julie to continue to keep a low profile while the police searched for her stalker.

"Yes, but you left shortly after dinner was over. You didn't even stay for dessert or the football game." Joe's dad finished while both parents took a seat.

"Joseph, stop chastising him. It's clear why, and no wonder he hasn't brought Julie to meet us either with you going on like this. You've got her nervous and looking like she's ready to bolt. Come sit by me, Julie."

Mrs. Bascomb patted the couch cushion. "My husband isn't blaming you for anything. He likes to have his kids and grandkids around him all the time and forgets sometimes they have other interests."

Julie gingerly perched on the couch next to Joe's mother. His father sat in one of the recliners and Joe sat in the other opposite him.

"Now don't go putting it all on me. Who was it that decided to take a drive this afternoon and drop by? You're the one that started speculating over Joe's brief phone calls and shortened visits."

"I only said we were overdue to come for a visit. Now hush up so I can talk to Julie."

"Now you're in for it, my dear. I hope you have your entire family history and life ready for a thorough discussion. Prepare for the interrogation."

"Joseph Anthony Bascomb! I do not interrogate. Is it so wrong to want to get to know the young lady our son is clearly smitten with?"

Julie glanced over at Joe for a clue on how to proceed. He sat leisurely in his chair with a smile on his face as he gazed back and forth between his parents. She guessed this must be normal behavior for them.

Joe's dad winked at her when she looked back between the two of them. He and his son shared more than just a name and the same-color eyes, apparently.

Adrienne tilted her head, smiled at her, and reached over to grasp Julie's hand, which rested on her leg. "Now, how long have you been dating?"

"Um, well..." Julie glanced at Joe beseechingly.

Why wasn't he saying anything? "We've only known each other a few weeks."

"Are you from Autumn Valley?"

"No, I live in Boston."

"Boston? How did you two meet?"

Once again, she glanced toward Joe. How did he want her to explain her current predicament to his parents? She didn't want to lie to them, but she hardly wanted to go into all the details either.

"Julie and I met at the Monarch Inn. She was a guest there. I repaired a few pieces of furniture for Kyle and had just finished dinner when she checked in."

"Oh, I love the Monarch Inn. Joseph and I stayed there for a romantic weekend once. The food in the Café was delicious." Adrienne turned to her husband. "Do you remember? We should go back for dinner sometime."

"I remember the new nightgown you wore for the trip. The food pales in comparison."

"Joseph!" Joe's mother shook her head and swung back to Julie with a slight blush on her cheeks.

A smile inched across Julie's mouth. Joe's parents were adorable. They obviously were still very much in love and their banter was charming. She eased back against the back of the couch with her hand still firmly grasped in Adrienne's.

"You were on vacation?"

"Does anyone want anything to eat or drink?" Joe stood up and glanced around the seated group.

"I'll have a beer."

Adrienne glanced sharply at her husband.

"What? I'm allowed an occasional beer."

She sighed and looked at Joe. "Just one."

He nodded. "What about you, Mom? Julie?"

"Water for me please."

Julie shook her head. Joe wandered into the kitchen to fetch his parents' drinks.

Adrienne smiled at Julie expectantly.

"Joe has told me a little about his nieces and nephews. How many grandchildren do you have?"

Her entire face lit up. "Six." She reached for her purse.

"My son, Anthony, has four children—Robert, Nicholas, Claudia, and little Elizabeth. Sophia, my daughter, has two—Michael and John."

Pulling out a small blue photo album, she opened it and showed Julie the pictures inside.

Joe returned with the drinks and sat back in the chair. His father and he started discussing football and whether The Patriots would win Sunday's game or not. Mrs. Bascomb continued to show Julie pictures with a little explanation of who was in the photo and where and when it was taken. Pride and love shown from her with the turn of every page. Joe was prominent throughout along with his brother, sister, and their spouses and children.

"Do you have any brothers or sisters?" Adrienne closed the photo album and tucked it back in her purse.

"No, I'm an only child."

"Why don't we see if we can make reservations for dinner at the Red Maple Café tonight? It will be our treat?" Joe's dad inserted the question casually.

Julie met Joe's gaze. "Maybe some other time. Why don't you and Mom stay for dinner here tonight? I was planning on making Grandma's recipe for Fettuccini Alfredo."

"We'd love to, wouldn't we Joseph?"

"Of course, but I thought it would be nice to take them out for dinner. And besides, you and I might see if the Monarch Inn has any vacancies tonight. We could stay overnight." Winking at his wife, he turned and smiled at Julie and Joe. "What do you say?"

"It's leaf peeping season. The inn is probably booked."

Joseph hesitated to take a sip of beer and glanced at his son. "Is there a particular reason you don't want to go to the inn?"

Julie winced. Joe was clearly at a loss for words. He was staring at his father silently. His mother kept glancing back and forth between them. Not wanting to be the one responsible for creating tension between Joe and his parents, Julie leaned forward. "It's my fault, Mr. Bascomb."

He gazed at her, waiting patiently for her to explain. She took a deep breath.

"No. It isn't." Joe scooted forward in his chair and rested his elbows on his knees. "Look, Julie has a stalker. That's why she left Boston and why she can't go to the inn. He or she tracked her there and broke into her room."

Adrienne inhaled sharply and squeezed Julie's hand. Joseph set his bottle of beer on the coffee table.

"What do the police say about this? Do they know who it is?"

Tears gathered in her eyes as Joe briefly told his parents what he knew. His mother scooted closer and wrapped an arm around Julie's shoulders, continuing to keep hold of the hand she already held. Instead of stiffening and pulling away, Julie relaxed against her, accepting the comfort she was trying to give. A pleasant and subtle floral perfume emanated from Adrienne.

"So she's been staying here with you?"

Joe nodded at his father.

"Good."

"I've been using the studio apartment in the barn."

"Do you think that's a good idea?" his mother queried softly.

Before Joe responded, his mother continued, "You should stay in the house with her. For safety, but also because I'm sure Julie must be terrified. I would be. Joseph, what can we do? There must be something we can do to help them."

Shocked by their easy acceptance and the immediate desire to help, Julie glanced back and forth between them. No wonder Joe was the same way.

"What if you took her to our home in Florida until they catch him?"

Joe stared at his father and then looked at Julie. "It's a thought. What do you think?"

Julie was momentarily speechless by their generosity.

Joseph stood. "I understand if the two of you want to discuss it in private. I'm sure you have a lot to consider. Why don't your mom and I get dinner started and leave you two alone?"

Adrienne rubbed her shoulder and patted Julie's hand before standing and taking the hand her husband held out. They disappeared into the kitchen together, and Joe relocated to take his mom's place beside her.

"It's not a bad idea."

No, it wasn't. Her stalker shouldn't be able to connect her to Joe, let alone his parents or their winter home.

"I'm not really sure what to think, except your parents are wonderful, and I can see how you turned out so great."

Joe grinned. "You think I'm great, huh?"

Julie laughed and settled her head on his shoulder. "Yes."

He wrapped an arm around her and pulled her close just as his cell phone rang. He leaned to the side to slip it from his pocket and check caller I.D. He glanced at her. "It's the sheriff."

Chapter Thirteen

Joe's face grew taut, and it sounded as if he was grinding his teeth. She couldn't hear the actual words being spoken by the sheriff, but by the cues his body gave out, the news wasn't good.

He pressed the button to disconnect the call and held the phone clenched in his fist as he stared at the floor. Maybe the news hadn't concerned her after all. The sheriff hadn't asked to speak to her. Had he received bad news unrelated to her?

Julie scooted closer to him and rubbed his back. "What is it?"

Sitting back, he returned his arm to its place around her shoulders, stroking her upper arm. "The Boston police said they got a call reporting a disturbance at your apartment. When they got there the T.V. was blasting." Julie stuffed her trembling hands under her thighs. Joe looked her way, but she couldn't meet his gaze. "Your apartment had been ransacked. Julie, they pretty much destroyed everything there, slashing cushions, smashing your furniture, shredding your clothes, holes in the walls."

He placed his other hand on her knee. She stared at the dark hair on the back of his hand. A few faded white scars crisscrossed across his knuckles.

"They think the stalker's behavior has escalated because they can't find you."

That was good in a way, wasn't it? The stalker didn't know where she was then. They had basically thrown an adult temper tantrum when they couldn't find their missing plaything. "No one was hurt, right?"

"No, and nobody claimed to see anything. Just reported the loud T.V. and what sounded like a fight. The police responded to what they thought was a domestic disturbance call."

Julie nodded as a tear trickled down her cheek.

"Awe, sweetheart, don't cry, we will get through this. They're going to catch them. They'll make a mistake. They're going through your apartment looking for fingerprints or DNA, anything to help identify who it is."

Joe gently wiped the tears from her cheeks. She was so tired. Tired of running. Tired of hiding. Tired of being afraid.

"We'll replace your things."

Shaking her head, she leaned against him. "They're just things."

Scooping her up into his arms, he placed her on his lap and wrapped his big arms around her. He rested his chin on top of her bent head as she snuggled against his chest.

Hesitant footsteps entered the living room and Joe shook his head at whoever stood there. The steps retreated into the kitchen.

A hiccupping sob escaped Julie as she dashed the tears from her face with the heel of her hand. When would it end?

"There's a bit of a silver lining here. The stalker doesn't know where you are and because he or she has committed felonies in two states not only are more law enforcement officials searching for him but the maximum sentence once they're caught has gone up."

"You're a glass half full guy, aren't you?"

"Absolutely."

Resting her head against his shoulder, Julie stared at the strong line of his jaw. Positivity had never been part of her personality. Not that she was negative—she preferred to think realistic. Even if they did catch the stalker, stalking and burglary would probably only get them a few years in prison unless they had prior offenses. She'd checked. Of course there was always parole for good behavior. Maybe she *was* focusing on the negative. It still meant they would be behind bars.

If they found the stalker and convicted him or her.

* * *

The haunted look was back in her eyes, and her skin was pale. The wounded air he noticed the first time he saw her had returned. Joe swallowed the rest of his drink and put the glass on the counter. The sound of the glass hitting the granite countertop rung throughout the kitchen causing Julie to flinch as she stood at the white farmhouse sink, next to his mother washing dishes. She had insisted on helping to clean up after dinner. He and his parents had tried to usher her into the living room, but she wouldn't listen.

Despite the delicious food his mother and father had prepared, dinner had been a relatively silent affair with only small bouts of inane small talk thrown in. He filled them in on the sheriff's call while Julie had gone upstairs to wash her face and try to pull herself together.

Joe leaned his hands on the countertop and hung his head. He wanted to fix this for her, but he didn't know how. The only feasible plan was to go with her to his parents' place in Florida. It was only a temporary solution, but what else could he do? If she stayed here, she would have to continue hiding. Her stalker knew she had been in Autumn Valley, but it didn't appear they knew she still was. If they left town, Julie would have a bit more freedom. Exactly for how long was up in the air. He could take a prolonged break from his business. It would require a little juggling, but it was manageable—however not indefinitely. He had savings but needed the income from making furniture to support himself.

Max laid curled up on the rug by the back door with his head resting on his paws, watching the activity in the kitchen. They would take him with them, of course, so he would only need someone to occasionally come by to check on his house and barn. Lucy, the barn cat, was fairly self-sufficient, but with the impending arrival of her kittens he would need to find someone to care for them while they were gone.

Dad walked back into the room from the bathroom and gave him a strong clap on the shoulder and a quick squeeze on the arm as he walked by. Mom glanced over her shoulder as he paused next to her and leaned down to kiss her on the cheek. Julie smiled slightly at the two of them as she dried the last of the dishes.

"I believe it's time for us to hit the road." Dad smiled sadly in his direction before turning to take Julie's hands in his. "Our door is always open to you. If you ever need a helping hand, or just someone to lend an ear, please come to us."

Julie smiled and nodded. "Thank you for dinner, and everything. Joe is a very lucky man to have the two of you for parents."

Raising and kissing her hand, he smiled at her and winked. "Well now, on that, pretty lady, we can agree."

Mom folded Julie in her arms as Dad ambled over to join Joe at the counter. "All I need to do is make a quick phone call and you can leave in an instant for the Florida house." His voice was low and his eyes grim. "Thanks, Dad."

His father nodded, and Joe escorted him to the front door with Julie and his mom trailing behind them arm and arm. He hugged his mother before they both left. He stood at the door until their taillights disappeared down the driveway and then faced Julie. She stood by the picture window in the living room facing the front of the house with her arms wrapped around her waist. The end of her ponytail rested on her shoulder. The blue tips of her hair stood out starkly against the white T-shirt she wore.

He searched his mind for something he could say or do to ease her worry, but he was coming up empty. She didn't need to hear empty platitudes or promises he had no idea how or if he would be able to keep them.

"I want to call my parents."

———

Julie perched on the side of the bed and stared at the cell phone in her hands. She ran through sentences in her mind repeatedly trying to figure out a way to tell her parents about the stalker as briefly and efficiently as possible. Rubbing her damp hand on her jean-clad thigh, she switched the phone to her opposite hand and then did the same with her other hand.

She struggled to remember the last time she had spoken to either of them and couldn't recall when.

Christmas perhaps?

Sighing, she dialed their home number and listened to it ring. Should she leave a message if they didn't pick up? What could she say? Joe had cautioned her to keep it brief and not tell them where she was. Even with the disposable phone she needed to be careful. What if the stalker was somehow listening to her parents' calls?

"Roy residence." The deep, scratchy voice brought a flood of memories rushing through her head of her father sitting in his office chair smoking a pipe and the sweet-smelling trail of smoke arising from the mouthpiece.

Julie let out a slow unsteady breath. "Hello, Dad."

"Julie?"

"Yes, it's me. How are you and Mom?"

"We're fine, fine. How are you?"

Opening her mouth to give the rote reply of fine, she sighed and closed her eyes. "Actually, that's why I'm calling. I've run into a bit of trouble."

"What kind of trouble?"

"It's kind of hard to explain."

"Do you need money?"

"No." Yeah, she did, but she hadn't accepted a dime from her parents since she turned eighteen, and she wasn't about to start now.

"Julie, tell me what's going on."

Rubbing her forehead, she drew a deep breath and let it out slowly. "I have a stalker. They've been harassing me for months with pictures, but now they escalated and burglarized my apartment, destroying everything."

"Where are you? At the police station? I'm coming to get you."

Shock immobilized her for a moment. He was coming to get her?

"Julie, tell me where you are." The command was clear in his tone, but so was the underlying concern.

"I can't do that at the moment."

"What do you mean?"

"Listen, Dad, I'm safe right now. It's all I can tell you. I'm calling because I'm worried the stalker might go to your house. I wanted you and Mom to know if anyone shows up looking for me or asking about me to call the police."

"Who is he?"

"I don't know. The police haven't been able to identify anyone yet."

"Are you under police protection?"

"I really can't answer any questions."

"I'll hire a private investigator and bodyguards. You should come home."

Tears spilled over her eyelashes and trickled down the side of her nose, dripping onto the hand resting on her thigh.

A creak of the floorboards alerted her to Joe's presence. He stood in the open doorway with his hands stuffed in his front pockets.

"Thank you, Dad. I have to go. I'll...I'll talk to you soon. Bye."

Ending the call, she sniffled and gave Joe a wobbly smile. "Well, that didn't go exactly like I planned."

Joe wandered over and sat on the edge of the bed next to her and took her hand in his. "Tell me."

"He offered to hire a private investigator and bodyguards. Told me to come home. He sounded upset and worried."

"He's your father. Of course he's worried."

"I told you we aren't close. The truth is we barely talk at all. I was raised mostly by nannies and not the fairy tale kind either. They weren't sweet old granny types who filled in the maternal role. I had three of them, and none of them would have won any child rearing awards. The worst of them used to lock me in a closet whenever I misbehaved or when she wanted to watch her soap operas without me around. When I was twelve, I begged to be sent away to boarding school to get away from my parents and the nanny."

"Did you ever tell your parents?"

Shaking her head, she stared at his thumb rubbing the back of her hand. "It was during the time when if they were in the same room together, they were screaming at one another. After my father left, my mother hired a new nanny. That one just treated me with total apathy. They reconciled after I left for boarding school. I think with me gone their marriage improved. The yelling stopped."

"Some people aren't meant to have kids, but it sounds like your father does care for you and wants to help you. Are you going to take him up on his offer?"

She glanced up at Joe. He stared at her waiting for her response. Did he want her to run to her parents? Had he had enough? Who could blame him?

"I think Florida is a safer choice. Granted I'm biased, I don't want you to leave me. Private investigators and bodyguards sound impressive, but your stalker is more likely to find you at your parents' house than here or in Florida. I'm not trying to scare you, just give an opinion." Joe's words saved her from wondering if he'd had enough.

Nodding, she studied his handsome face. He should be pushing her to go to her parents—any sane person would. Was it the damsel in distress scenario that appealed to him? Did he get off on saving someone?

There went her negativity again. Joe wasn't like that. He was too good and decent. Anyone could see he was a sweetheart of a man.

Max wandered in and sat next to her, leaning against her leg. She reached down to give him a pat.

"I'm not going to my parents."

Joe let out a loud sigh. "Good. I'll call my dad and tell him we're leaving for Florida. I can have everything tied up here tomorrow and then we can go."

Squeezing Joe's hand, she stared out the window. The rain had slowed to a drizzle. The white eyelet curtains were probably his mother's choice, and they fit perfectly with the blue and white quilt covering the bed they sat on. The style was homey and comforting. It wasn't something she probably would have chosen a month ago. Her apartment was decorated in an eclectic, colorful mishmash of shabby chic. At least it had been.

"I'm not going to Florida either."

Twisting on the bed and dragging her knee up to face Joe, Julie frowned and shook her head. "Fear has driven me for so long. I've made every decision based on fear. I don't want to live that way anymore. I'm done with running."

Chapter Fourteen

wo barks from downstairs drew Julie's attention from spraying the latest sketch of Joe so it wouldn't smudge. It depicted him sanding a chest of drawers. She'd drawn it while watching him work in his barn this morning. This was the seventh drawing she'd done of him. Julie had never drawn someone more than twice, and the only time she had sketched a man she was dating was when he had asked her to. Something to think about.

Later.

Silence from the kitchen pulled her to the hallway. She had thought Max barked to announce Joe coming in for lunch, but Joe always called to her when he came in.

"Max?" Julie walked to the top of the stairs and stared down. She thought she heard him whine and started down the stairs. He probably needed to go out.

As she rounded the corner at the bottom of the stairs, strong arms wrapped around her from behind. A purple latex-shrouded hand covered her mouth. The noxious odor from the gloves and stale body sweat filled her nostrils and made her gag.

Struggling for release, her gaze landed on Max lying still on the kitchen floor. *Oh God, was he dead?*

She kicked back at whoever was holding her. A black sneaker-clad foot appeared in her line of vision as her attacker struggled to maintain their balance. She stomped down hard on the shoe, but other than a muffled swear from behind her head, her bare feet appeared to do little damage.

Chomping down with her teeth on the hand across her mouth, she managed to gain enough freedom to move one of her arms. Julie made a fist and struck back with every ounce of strength she had.

A soft grunt preceded her momentary release.

Before she could take a step, her attacker clutched her head in their hands and slammed her against the wall of the kitchen.

Her vision blurred as pain exploded in her head. Her balance failed her, and she clutched at empty air for purchase.

"Why did you make me do that?"

The words permeated her brain, and she looked up at the source, but before she could see her attacker clearly, he grabbed her once again and dragged her farther into the kitchen. She opened her mouth to scream for help, but nausea churned in her stomach and bile rose as the room tilted and spun.

He shoved her into the kitchen closet under the stairs.

The door slammed shut and darkness surrounded her.

The scrape of a chair against the floor sounded through the wood. The door shuddered briefly as something hit it from the other side.

Panic stole her breath. She was locked in a closet. Max was most likely dead.

Where was Joe? Was he totally unaware of what was happening? Or worse? Had her stalker found him in the barn?

Her chest shuddered with labored breaths.

She scooted back until her spine hit the wall, and she wrapped her arms around her folded knees. Hiccupping sobs thundered through her.

The terror of her childhood locked for hours on end in a dark closet lashed at her mind.

She rocked back and forth.

A bang against the door sounded above her head.

"Why, why, why?"

Another thud against the door.

Julie's body shook. She took several big gulping breaths.

"We're meant to be together. You'll see. You shouldn't have run from me. You shouldn't have rejected my gifts. You shouldn't have chosen him. You're mine!"

The rage in his voice battled with a terrifying whining quality. Julie squeezed her eyes tightly closed and prayed for someone to help her.

"I'm going to fix this. You'll see. Everything will be as it's supposed to be. I'll make you understand. Once we're alone together, everything will be fine."

The shuffle of feet grew distant. Julie opened her eyes. Her teeth clattered together so hard pain pulsed in her jaw.

Silence stretched, and her trembling body ached. Was he gone? Who was he? What gifts? The pictures? Did he think terrorizing her was a form of courting?

Light filtered in from underneath the door. It wasn't completely dark. Shadowed shapes surrounded her. Blinking rapidly to force her eyes to adjust to the darkened interior, she searched the closet. A dusty smell coated with the stringent aroma of bleach lingered in the air.

Where was the vacuum, broom, and box of cleaners? He'd emptied the closet beforehand. He had planned to stuff her in here. Why?

She placed her hands on the floor and shifted sideways to listen at the door.

Nothing except her harsh breathing.

Wiping her wet cheeks and dribbling nose, she took several deep, calming breaths. *Think, why would he lock her in here?*

Was he searching the house? She listened intently for sounds from upstairs. There were no footsteps, no creaking floorboards or stairs. Was he coming back for her?

Julie searched the closet space for anything she might use as a weapon.

Nothing.

She listened again for any sound, but only silence greeted her. Had he left? No, he had said they would be alone together.

Should she bang on the door and scream for help or would that bring him back sooner?

Where was Joe?

Had her attacker gone after Joe in the barn? Had that been what he meant by fixing this?

Julie scrambled to her feet and traced her fingers along the edges of the door. She tore her nails trying to shove the pins from the brackets, hoping to free the door from the hinges and escape.

It was no use. Without some sort of tool, she couldn't budge them.

She threw her weight against the door, once, twice, three times. All to no avail. She ran her palms over the smooth walls, hoping to find a forgotten nail or screw to use to pry open the hinges.

Her hand hovered over the sheetrock. Could she break through the plaster?

Using the side of her clenched fist she punched the wall next to the door approximately midway up where the handle should be. The sheetrock dented and then split after repeated blows. She made a hole. Wires fastened to wood with large staples ran along the inside of the doorframe. She pushed and punched against the outer sheetrock.

Light shown through the cracks as the sheetrock gave way. She bent and peered through the hole to see a chair wedged under the door handle. She needed to make the hole bigger to reach the chair.

Covered in white sheetrock dust by the time she managed to stretch far enough to pry the chair out of the way, Julie grasped the handle and opened the door. Her hands were scratched, bleeding, and sore but she was free of the closet.

She ran to Max still lying on the floor. A sob shook her frame until she saw the slight movement of his abdomen. He was alive, but she didn't know for how long.

Looking toward the barn, she whispered, "I'm sorry boy, but I have to find Joe first."

She took several steps toward the back door before turning and running to the phone on the wall. *Please work.*

Lifting the receiver, she listened for the dial tone. When it buzzed in her ear, she released the breath she had been holding. She dialed 911 and rattled off the Red Clover Road address to the dispatcher. "I've been attacked. The stalker broke into the house. He hurt Max, the dog. I don't know where Joe is. He was working in the barn."

The dispatcher calmly replied. "Police are on the way. Please stay on the line."

Julie dropped the receiver. It bounced off the wall and dangled by the cord. Waiting wasn't an option. She had to find Joe.

Opening the back door, she sprinted across the backyard. As she neared the barn, she noticed the door to Joe's workshop was open. He never left the door open. He kept it closed to protect the wood from moisture.

She barreled through the open door without an inkling of caution.

Crashes echoed from the loft above where Joe's apartment was. She ran for the stairs. A shovel hanging on the wall captured her attention. She paused long enough to rip it from the holder and clenched the handle in her fist.

A crackling sounded in her ears over the pounding of her heart.

She stepped onto the landing and stopped short in the open doorway. Joe was on the ground. Wires spread from his leg and abdomen. His body jerked in some type of spasm. Her gaze tracked the wires to their source.

A man, dressed in a black hoodie, baseball cap, and jeans, stood across the room with a taser in his hand. His pale skin was ruddy and damp from exertion.

Shock held Julie immobile.

A spark of recognition teased her brain, but she couldn't place him.

He leaped toward her.

She jumped backward landing against the doorjamb. Remembering the shovel, she swung it up and high over her head grasping it with two hands.

Julie swung with all her strength just as he reached for her.

A solid thwack rent the air as the shovel collided with his head, knocking the baseball cap off.

The man crumbled—his body hitting the floor with a loud thud. A trickle of blood seeped from his light brown hairline. She stared at the pale features desperately trying to place him.

Sirens echoed in the distance and propelled her to move. She edged around the body of her attacker with the shovel still clenched in her hand and dropped down next to Joe as he struggled to rise.

A shudder raced through her.

Should she remove the wires? What was the protocol? She hesitantly held her hand over him not knowing what to do.

He grasped her free hand as his gaze remained locked on their attacker.

The sirens grew louder, and colored lights cast spinning shadows on the walls.

Julie stood and shouted, "In here! He's hurt! Please hurry!"

The sound of pounding feet echoed in the workshop below.

She kneeled beside Joe once again, slipping her hand into one of his. He had pushed himself to a sitting position against the bed and pulled the wires from his body. He took the shovel from her hand and held it in his.

She yelled once again, "Up here. Please hurry!"

The police called out and identified themselves as they ran up the stairs. Two uniformed officers appeared in the opening with guns drawn. Their experienced gazes took in the situation in a glance. One of them spoke into a radio attached to his shoulder requesting an ambulance.

Sheriff Bennett entered the room next. Her gaze darted first to Joe and then the stalker. A groan preceded the man's lurching movement.

"I hit him with the shovel."

The police cuffed the stalker as he struggled against them. His crazed gaze landed on Julie as they dragged him to a standing posi-tion. She raised her chin and met his gaze, with only a slight tremble in her chin. Once the police escorted him out the doorway and out of sight, she turned her head into Joe's shoulder and sobbed.

Chapter Fifteen

The heat of the coffee warmed her chilled hands as Julie wrapped them around the mug. The familiar aroma comforted her, and she held the cup closer. She sat in the corner of Joe's couch while he hovered above her with one hand on her shoulder.

The state police had left, and the sheriff was in the process of following behind them. Julie had answered round after round of questions throughout the afternoon. Her mind was blank.

They'd allowed her a break to shower and change her clothes. Her damp hair curled against her neck after she tucked it behind her ears. The thick gray borrowed sweater she wore did little to warm her chilled skin.

They had informed her of her stalker's identity — Steve Brown, a temporary technician her company had hired almost a year ago. That's how he had gotten access to her work computer. She had a vague recollection of possibly seeing him once in the stairwell of her office building, but she wasn't sure. She didn't remember ever speaking a word to him. What had caused him to fixate on her?

"Julie?"

She lifted her head and met the sheriff's sympathetic gaze.

"He'll be going away for a long time. It's attempted kidnapping and murder now. You're safe."

Julie nodded and forced a semblance of a smile to curve her lips. The stalker had overheard an innocent comment in town about Joe's new girlfriend with the blue hair which had led him straight to Joe's door.

She tensed as the door opened and closed when the sheriff left. Forcing herself to remain still and not swing around in panic to watch for movement behind her, she fought her fear.

Joe walked in front of her and eased down next to her on the couch. He put his arm around her, and she snuggled into his side.

The veterinarian had called and said Max should make a full recovery, but they were keeping him overnight for observation.

She'd called her parents earlier to let them know she was all right, and the stalker was caught. They had asked her once again to come home. She promised to visit in a few days once everything had settled down. Forming a stronger relationship with her parents was something they would have to work on, but for the first time she thought it possible.

Joe had called and talked to his parents also. Joseph and Adrienne had wanted to rush over, but he'd convinced them to wait a bit until things had settled down. At the time, the police had still roamed the property collecting evidence.

He hadn't left her side the entire afternoon. Joe refused to go to the hospital to be thoroughly checked out after being tasered. He'd waited outside the bathroom door while she showered and dressed, only taking a couple of minutes to change his own clothes.

"Is there anything I can do for you?"

She glanced at his profile. The beginning of a bruise crept underneath his eye. "Just hold me for a while."

"That I can do."

"We should put ice on that bruise." She pointed toward his face while he shook his head.

"It's nothing."

"I'm sorry." They both said in unison.

Joe frowned. "Why are you sorry?"

"Because I almost got you killed!"

He snorted. "You did no such thing. In fact, I seem to recall a wild woman swinging a shovel coming to my rescue and saving me from a lunatic."

A smile wobbled across her face. "Why are you sorry?"

"I promised to protect you. Instead, I let him get to you."

Reaching up, she cupped his jaw in her hand. "Joe, you have protected me again and again. You took me in, practically a complete stranger. You made me feel safe and cared for. You kept me sane in the middle of the insanity."

Joe cradled her hand with his own. "I love you. I think I started falling in love with you the first moment I laid eyes on you at the inn."

Just when she thought she had no tears left to shed her eyes filled up again.

"You don't have to say anything back now. I know I probably should have waited. You've been through so much today. I've been bursting with the words for days, and I didn't want to wait any longer to say them to you. If today has taught me anything it's you never know what tomorrow will bring. I don't want to wait anymore. I want to make it clear how I feel. I love you and want you in my life, Julie. I want you to be my wife."

She swallowed hard.

"I realize this isn't the most romantic proposal, but I promise I'll make it up to you if you'll let me." "I don't know, it sounded pretty romantic to me."

Joe grinned, and those irresistible dimples appeared. He leaned down and seized her lips in a passionate kiss.

Julie raised her other hand to cup both his cheeks. Staring into his eyes, an overwhelming tide of emotion filled her. "I love you too."

Joe gave her a quick kiss and then stood and scooped her up into his arms. Laughing, she grabbed hold of his shoulders.

"What are you doing?"

"I'm taking you upstairs where I can hold you properly and show you how much hearing you say those words means to me."

Joe paused on the bottom step and gazed down. "Unless it's too soon. I don't want to push you. I'll be perfectly happy holding you in my arms all night."

"I won't. We've waited long enough, don't you think? Besides, I can think of nothing better to cleanse the ugliness of today than making love with the man I love."

Grinning, he climbed the stairs with her in his arms. He hesitated as he stepped over the threshold to his bedroom. "Not to press, but does this mean you'll marry me? I can carry you over the threshold wearing a wedding dress?"

Her breath caught in her throat. The image of Joe in a tuxedo holding her in his arms while she wore a white wedding dress flashed into her mind and lingered.

"I wouldn't want to disappoint your parents. I think they may have already named our children."

Joe threw his head back and laughed. "You're probably right."

He placed her on the bed with his hands on either side of Julie, supporting his weight as he leaned over her. "I've waited a long time for you, Julie Roy."

"And I've waited my whole life for you, Joe Bascomb."

About the Author

Denise Carbo writes immersive, happily-ever-after Romance and Women's Fiction with a touch of humor and suspense. She is a voracious reader and loves to travel.

She lives in a small, picturesque, New England town with her high school sweetheart and their three amazing sons. Find out more at https://www.DeniseCarbo.com and sign up for her newsletter to be the first to hear about new books, giveaways, and exclusive content. https://eepurl.com/dt5N7M

Also by Denise Carbo

Bloodlines

Clan. Duty. Love. Which will he choose?

They have been here for centuries. War destroyed their planet, and now they hide among us. Malcolm Donovan, a dragon shifter, rules over one of four clans. When a clan member is murdered, he must find the killer. Nothing will disrupt his pledge to protect his clan. Nothing that is until he finds his mate.

Elsie Monroe, human to the bone, and the resort manager for the Donovan family finds herself falling in love with the charming Wyoming town, and she can't help but be drawn to the mysterious Malcolm Donovan. His rude attitude is atrocious, but his kisses can bring chocolate to a boiling point. Not to mention what he does to her body and heart.

Soon Elsie is dragged into a world of secrecy and violence. Creatures she thought were fantasy are actually real. And she is left wondering if love will be enough to capture and tame her own personal dragon.

Guilt & Redemption

Allison is a widow with dark secrets. Nightmares plague her nights. Guilt and shame shadow her days. Her new neighbor sparks feelings she thought shriveled and dead.

Jim's temporary lifestyle of renovating a house, selling it, and moving on doesn't leave room for relationships—and that's just the way he likes it. His new neighbor is not his type, but he's drawn to her anyway.

Allison's past won't stay buried. Trust is a precious commodity. Revenge, truth, and justice all have two sides. Will Allison and Jim find themselves on opposing sides?

My First My Last My Only

A second chance at love or heartbreak…

Socially awkward and prone to accidents, Franny Dawson has a brand-new project—herself. Owning the local bakery, The Sweet Spot, has taken all her time and energy and she's neglected the social aspects of her life. The small lakeside town of Granite Cove, New Hampshire is full of quirky residents eager to help and hinder her new plan.

Mitch Atwater, her first love, returns to town. He has an agenda of his own and is wreaking havoc with her goals and her heart.

Can Franny outwit her nemesis, overcome her perfect sister's surprise return, and escape the cocoon of her own insecurities to take a chance on love and get her very own happily ever after?

Covet thy Neighbor

Serial killer or new love interest...

Single mom of twin boys, Olivia Banner, has her hands full juggling life's demands. She doesn't have time for her mysterious new neighbor or all the questions his presence conjures up, even if he is a handsome devil.

Toss in a complicated relationship with her ex-husband, meddlesome family members, and going back to school to provide a stable financial future for her and her boys, and Olivia turns to her gal pals for guidance.

Sometimes playing it safe is the right choice, and other times leaping into the unknown can lead to all the dreams you never knew you had coming true.

No Choice at All

One night. One choice. Changes everything.

One single moment can change a person's life forever. Moving to Granite Cove was supposed to be Rebecca's fresh start. She has a firm no dating rule. There's no time or room in her life—*and* she has horrible taste in men.

One impulsive decision threatens all her careful planning. Ian, the handsome stranger she never thought she'd see again, keeps showing up and weakening her resolve.

Love is a fairy tale only the young and naïve believe in. Can Ian change her mind and heart and teach her to trust?

Whispers & Broken Promises

Dumped and deserted…

Instead of the proposal she expected, Tina's boyfriend dumps her and moves across the country. She's left behind questioning her future and what went wrong.

A handsome single dad moves to town and the complications multiply.

She's spent her entire existence in the small lakeside town of Granite Cove, New Hampshire. Besides knowing every detail of her life, the residents feel it's only right they help her decide how she should live the rest of it.

A Yearning Dilemma

Kelly yearns for a family connection despite being surrounded by siblings, parents, and extended relations. She let chance choose her destiny and ended up in Granite Cove searching for a home.

A contrary celebrity ensnares her in the turmoil embroiling his life and makes her question all her choices.

Christmas is the season of miracles and forgiveness, but how do you choose between family, friends, career, and love? And why do you have to?

A Change in Perspective

What do you do when your perfect life blows up in your face? Move home to Granite Cove and hope you can put some of the pieces back together. Except what if the pieces no longer fit?

Lucinda reevaluates her life decisions and realizes many of her choices don't paint a pretty picture. She's determined to put her people pleasing habits behind her and discover the life she's meant to live.

She's known Bobby all her life—at least she thought she did. He keeps showing up at all the wrong times and making his dislike of her crystal clear.

Secrets and lies. Responsibilities and expectations. Betrayal and loss. Can love really heal all wounds?